EIGHT MULES FROM MONTEREY

EIGHT MULES FROM MONTEREY

BY PATRICIA BEATTY

William Morrow and Company
New York   1982

Printed in the United States of America.
1   2   3   4   5   6   7   8   9   10

Library of Congress Cataloging in Publication Data

Beatty, Patricia.
    Eight mules from Monterey.
    Summary: During the summer of 1916 thirteen-year-old Fayette and her brother accompany their widowed mother on a mule trip into the California mountains, where she is to establish library outposts in isolated communities.
    [1. Libraries—Fiction. 2. California—Fiction. 3. The West—Fiction] I. Title.
PZ7.B380544Ei   [Fic]   81-22284
ISBN 0-688-01047-4   AACR2

For my Monterey friend Dorothy Smith,
who actually knew the fabulous Anne Hadden.

1

Not any one of us Ashmores—Eubie, Mother, or I,
Fayette—will ever forget that summer we got mixed up
with all those mules, the wild mountain man, and the
moonshiners who were shooting at us. No, there can't
ever be a summer like the summer of 1916 for any of
us again!

Our adventures started easy, with me fibbing to the
rich twin sisters Gladys and Thelma Hillman. I'd
walked home with them one day toward the end of May
only because we were all going the same way. I sort of
hoped that they would invite me in to see their big
house, the one with the best view of Monterey Bay in
town, and offer me some lemonade and cookies or whatever rich kids ate after school to keep their strength up.
But the twins didn't ask me in. They went up to their
fancy iron front gate, walked through it, and shut it.
Standing behind it, they looked at me and smiled.

"We have to go in now, Fayette, and practice the vio-
lin and piano," Gladys said. "Say, where are you spend-
ing the summer?"

Thelma didn't even wait for me to tell her "nowhere." She said, "Our Grandmother Hillman, who lives
on Nob Hill in San Francisco, is going to take us to Cape

Cod. She wanted to take us to Europe to tour Germany, France, England, and Italy, but those countries are still fighting a war. If we went over there, our ship might be sunk by submarines. So it's Cape Cod instead."

Gladys said, "Uh-huh, Cape Cod in June. That's in Massachusetts. We'll go all the way across the United States on a train."

To Massachusetts? I wasn't going anywhere at all, and they were going all the way to the other side of the country! I felt slightly sick as I looked at their white silk dresses, white silk stockings, their new white shoes, their pale blue taffeta sashes and matching hair bows, and their long auburn sausage curls. Someone obviously had the time to twine them over her fingers every morning to make them fat and jiggly.

My dress was white too, but it was only muslin. My shoes were old black ones that had been Mother's. I had no sash, and my long, straight hair was plain old brown, tied back with a black grosgrain ribbon. Yes, and my everyday eyes were dark brown, not pale, cool blue like theirs.

Oh, those rich-kid Hillmans! Every day in the week was a party day for them.

Thelma said, "Uh-huh, all the way on a train. What will you do this summer? Won't your mama be graduating out of that old library school by the time our school is over?"

"Yes, she'll be out of it."

I didn't add that Mother, a widow for three years now, didn't have a job after the library school let her out. The city library, which ran the school, didn't usually hire the people it trained. I knew she was worrying plenty about not having a job, but that wasn't any business of the Hillman twins. I stared at the two of them, who got noticed by everybody all the time not only because they were twins but because they had such nifty clothes, a big, fancy house, servants, and two Packard touring cars.

Gladys asked, "Well, where will you Ashmores go this summer?"

All at once I blurted out, thinking of their last name, "Oh, we're going to the hills!" One lie led to another. "Mother wanted to take us to the Swiss Alps, but she says too that we can't travel in Europe in wartime."

Oh, what a big pair of fibs those two were!

Thelma said, bug-eyed, "The Swiss Alps? I didn't know librarians made that much money or went to such interesting places. We want to go to the Swiss Alps someday too. We just read *Heidi*. It's about them."

I didn't tell them that I had read *Heidi* recently too, and that book was exactly where I'd got the idea for my whopping lie about the Alps. I said, "Well, we'll go to the Canadian Rockies instead."

The Rockies were every bit as romantic as Cape Cod and in a foreign country too. I added, "Of course, we'll go there on a train. Librarians just love to ride on trains. Well, I have to go now and get the special thread Mother wants to finish the midnight-blue georgette dress she's making for me. She's letting me wear long skirts in Canada. Good-bye."

Those were more big lies. I didn't know enough librarians to have any idea if they loved trains or not.

9

There was no long dress; I was still in short skirts like all thirteen-year-old girls. Mother couldn't sew worth a hoot. My real errand for her was to get a ball of twine, not thread.

Feeling choked up with unhappiness, I looked at Monterey Bay, sparkling in the sunshine. Monterey was a vacation place for people who came to exclaim about its history, old buildings, and lovely sites, but it wasn't a vacation spot for me, who lived there year round. Oh, how I wished I could go somewhere that summer too! Anywhere but Monterey would do.

Because of the Hillmans, I had no appetite for supper and let my pork chops get cold on my plate. Mother did all the talking at the table. She seemed in good spirits to-night, though I couldn't see why, when we were sort of poor. Having Father die so suddenly had changed each of our lives, but probably hers changed the most, be-cause now she had to think about how to earn a living for all of us. We'd had plenty of money when he was alive, but after she paid off his debts and her tuition to the library school, only our house and some furniture were left.

As I looked at her, I thought for the hundredth time that I sure didn't resemble her. My ten-year-old brother, Eubie, did. He had the yellow, curling hair, dark blue eyes, and slim body of her family. I was pure, chunky Ashmore, and if I didn't watch, I would someday run to fat.

Mother's eyes met mine as she started on the rice pud-ding dessert. Then she looked at Eubie and asked, "Do you two want to hear something very exciting? The county sheriff drove over to the library today from Salinas. He had a letter for the head of the library, Mr. Wallace."

Eubie asked, "Isn't that the postman's job to deliver letters?" How smart alecky he could be.

Mother told him, "Be quiet, Eubie. The letter wasn't really for him. It was for a library, and he brought it to us. It came from the 'desperate ladies' of Big Tree Junction, who wanted the services of a library. It seems they didn't quite know where to write, so they wrote the sheriff!"

To be polite, I asked, "What makes the ladies 'desperate'?"

"They are desperate for books, Fayette. The letter was signed by five ladies who have not had any new books to read for years. They wrote that the six books they do have are tattered, dog-eared, and falling to bits, because they have been read so much."

"Desperate for *books*?" Eubie shot me one of his fish-eyed looks that let me know he couldn't see how anyone could feel that way.

In spite of my sad personal feelings, I warmed somewhat to those five ladies. Having only six books to read for years could make anybody feel desperate. I was a classy reader for my age. "Has anybody ever been to Big Tree Junction?" I asked Mother. "You didn't say where it was."

"Mr. Wallace was there once on a fishing trip years ago. He called us all in today to tell us about the letter, and when I asked where it was, he said Big Tree

11

Junction is forty miles from Monterey, forty miles straight up."

"Straight up, Mother?"

"Well, practically straight up, Fayette. Big Tree Junction is in mountain country south of Monterey." I saw that she was looking dreamily over the rim of her teacup. Her voice had changed from brisk to gentle. "I've never been in the mountains, but I've often wondered what they would be like. I was born in flat Kansas, married in flat Iowa, and came straight out to California as a bride to flat Sacramento where your father set up his first law office. Then he came here to Monterey and set up his second office with his partner, Mr. Herbert." Then she added quickly, "Well, I won't be the one taking library books to the ladies of Big Tree Junction. Mr. Wallace told us he is sending Mr. Embleton."

Mr. Embleton! I knew him by sight—a stout, old wheezer, the number-two man in charge of the city library.

Eubie said with a snort, "Mr. Embleton? I don't think he could get forty miles up into the air. Mr. Wallace shouldn't send an old gink like him."

Mother nodded. "I don't think he should send a man of his age and portliness either, but he is the only other man the library employs."

The next day my eighth-grade teacher, Miss Uffelman, sent me to the library to get a certain little book of short stories for her to read from aloud. She'd just finished a long one by Robert Louis Stevenson, who had once lived in Monterey, and now she wanted a short book.

Speak of the devil, the first person I saw at the library was Mr. Embleton. I told him, "My teacher wants the book by Edgar Allan Poe that has the story 'The Fall of the House of Usher' in it. She says you have it here. She says it wakes sleepy kids up because it's got some action in it."

Mr. Embleton nodded, wheezed, and said, "I presume your teacher is Effie Uffelman? She asks for the Poe book regularly this time of year. I hear that she carries on considerably when she reads that tale about the lady who gets buried alive. It's quite a spine-chilling story. She says that the shrieking is wonderfully helpful to her nervous system at the end of the school year."

"Spine chilling." That sounded nifty. I asked, "Is the book in? She wants it now."

"Yes, I shelved it this morning. It's a whole collection of Poe tales, not just the one story she wants. Do you know Poe, little girl?"

"Of course not! He died back before the Civil War started, but I know his poem 'The Raven.' I'd recite it for you, but I guess my teacher's waiting to chill our spines."

I watched him get up, leave his desk, and lumber to a big wall filled with books. A ladder stood there, propped against the bookcase.

He'd been very nice to me, helpful and polite the way Mother said librarians ought to be to patrons. What interesting things he'd said about Miss Uffelman! I wished

Mother was there so I could tell her, but she wasn't around. She was in the rear of the building, out of sight, being taught how to be a librarian by Mr. Wallace.

I kept my eyes on Mr. Embleton as he went up the ladder and reached for a skinny black book on the top shelf of the bookcase. Just as he got his hand on it, the ladder slid sideways. Mr. Embleton dropped the book and tried to grab hold of a shelf with his hands, but down went the ladder with a crash and down went Mr. Embleton with it, tangled up in its rungs. I gasped. The "Fall of the House of Usher" had been his downfall.

As he lay on the floor groaning, a door was flung open and out ran bushy-headed Mr. Wallace crying out to me, "What's wrong here?"

I pointed to Mr. Embleton on the floor and said, "He fell. He was getting a book for me from the top shelf." I stooped, picked up the book, and said, "Here it is. I'm sorry."

How exasperated Mr. Wallace looked as he glanced from me to Mr. Embleton. I kept quiet in case he might be angry. He didn't know me by sight, because I never pestered Mother. Last year I'd been one of his wife's pupils. She was my seventh-grade teacher. I had been her "pet," as a matter of fact, but he didn't know that. I backed away from him with the book in my hands, as he stretched out both of his to Mr. Embleton, then drew them back and said, "No, you stay where you are, Embleton. I'll call for the doctor to come over."

He hurried off, while library workers and other patrons crowded around to stare. I bent over again and picked up Mr. Embleton's eyeglasses, gave them back to him, and said, "I'm sorry, but they busted when you fell."

He looked at one of the library workers, not me, and said, "Minna, I don't think I'll be traveling up through the hills to Big Tree Junction now. I think I have been saved by the grace of Edgar Allan Poe."

As I went away to check out the book, I wondered what he meant by that. How had Edgar Allan Poe saved him when Poe had died before the Civil War started?

Naturally, I asked Mother that night how Mr. Embleton was. She said, "He didn't break any bones, but he is badly bruised and in bed at home. Mr. Wallace is very perturbed about the accident. He can't send Embleton to the hills now. Perhaps he will have to go in his place. He has already mailed a letter to the desperate women of Big Tree Junction, saying they can count on someone from the library honoring their request for books. But Mr. Wallace really can't spare the time to go."

I said, "Then let him send a lady librarian. Let him send *you!*" The words just sprang out of me without thinking.

Mother grinned at me and said, "Fayette, I'm not a librarian yet. I won't be until I am graduated from the library school. But it isn't as if I wouldn't be willing."

Eubie told her, "But you say you'll get out of that old school by the end of this week. Hey, why *can't* you go to Big Tree Junction in place of old Embleton or Wallace?"

Mother told him wistfully, "It's a nice thought, and thank you for it, but I believe Mr. Wallace will look for some man who is not a librarian to go with the books and with instructions from the library. I very much doubt if Mr. Wallace would consider sending a female librarian with the mule driver he hired the other day to accompany Mr. Embleton. He is the one who will tend the horses and the mules. I have heard he is called Murfree, Mr. Denver Murfree."

"Horses?" breathed Eubie, who doted on them the way most Monterey boys doted on automobiles. "Will horses pull the wagons or will mules?"

"Neither, Eubie. There are no wagon roads in the mountains. They are far too steep for roads. The horses, I presume, will be ridden, and the mules will carry a lending library in their saddlebags."

Books on mules? Now that was exciting, I told myself. As exciting as the Canadian Rockies. I could just see us galloping into Big Tree Junction on pure white steeds, followed by pack mules. People would run cheering from every direction and be very grateful to us. We would be welcomed like heroes, something that wouldn't happen to the Hillmans on Cape Cod.

I asked, "Mother, how long would the trip take?"

"Some weeks. The time depends on a number of factors."

I took a deep breath. "Mother, you say Mr. Wallace may have to hire somebody who's not from the library. Why should he have to do that? *You* go ask him for the job. You're athletic enough to do it. It isn't as if you'd be walking, carrying books on your back. While you're at it, ask him if Eubie and I can go too." I was thinking fast, as fast as I had when I'd lied to the Hillman sisters yesterday.

Eubie could think fast too, at times. He said, "Sure, Mr. Wallace won't have to pay us money to help you. If we all go, you won't have to pay anybody to stay here with us and keep house while you're away."

Mother put down the stocking she was darning and said, frowning, "I don't know, children. It would be a new sort of venture for me. I have never camped out before in my life. I have no breeches or boots to wear in the mountains."

I said, "You can buy them, Mother."

She sighed. "Children, I very much doubt if our good friend Mr. Herbert would approve of this idea. I can just imagine what he would say. Mr. Wallace would be the first to object, though." She shook her head. "Fayette, for some reason Mr. Embleton didn't at all look forward to going. He said that you, the little girl who asked him for the Poe book, were an agent of Providence, someone who saved him by her request for the book on the top shelf."

I asked, "Providence? What's that?"

"Fate. The hand of God."

Glory be. I had never thought of myself that way before. What a compliment!

I got my second compliment of the day from her when I went to bed that night. Mother was going too, and she stopped on the stair landing beside me to say, "Fayette, I waited to talk to you till Eubie had gone up to bed. I think you are old enough now for us to talk woman to woman."

That stopped me in my tracks. "Yes, Mother?"

She was frowning the "family frown" she shared with

Eubie. "Fayette, Mr. Herbert asked me to marry him last Sunday. He has given me till the end of the summer to give him my answer. He's really pressing me for a reply. I didn't tell you or Eubie before, but Mr. Herbert has already asked me twice this year to marry him."

I said, "Tell him No. Nobody ought to be pressed!"

I didn't take to Father's sobersides old law partner, who acted like he owned us when he came to our house. Lately he even started calling Eubie "son" and Eubie didn't like it. Eubie's first name was Herbert, and he sure didn't want to be Herbert Herbert. Now I saw why the word *son* was used. Mr. Herbert had it in mind to be our stepfather, and soon. I didn't.

Mother said, "Everybody tells me he is a very good catch and will be a good provider for us. I don't want to worry you, Fayette, but I need to work. I have to. I need somehow to be hired by the library when I graduate. They haven't offered me any position yet. Maybe they expect me to move to some other city to find work. It isn't their custom to hire their own students. I think we may have to sell the house and leave."

"But this is our home! I don't want to leave it. You and Dad built this house."

"Yes, but I still may have to sell it and live off the proceeds until I find work elsewhere."

"No, Mother! You ask for the Big Tree Junction job like Eubie and I asked you to. I bet if you get that and do okay, you'll be working for the library here this fall, and we'll hang onto the house and stay in Monterey."

"Fayette, I *do* plan to ask for the mountain job." How she was glaring at the newel post! "I have another

18

reason for wanting it also. If I don't see Mr. Herbert for a while, I'll have time alone to consider his offer of marriage." And she went up ahead of me, leaving me to pull the dangling chain that turned out the light bulb.

At the top of the steps, I vowed that I would do everything I could to help Mother get the job. Glory be, tomorrow could be an interesting day with Mother asking for the job and Miss Uffelman letting herself go in the chilling spots of the Poe story.

It *was* an interesting day. Miss Uffelman didn't disappoint me. She did a good bit of shrieking, acting out "The Fall of the House of Usher" while reading it aloud. My, but Mr. Edgar Allan Poe could make a person's hair stand straight on end!

After school let out for the day, I hurried to beat Mother home. Eubie arrived only a minute or so later, and as I let him in the front door, he asked, "Have you heard anything yet about Mother and the Big Tree Junction job?"

"No, I didn't dare go to the library today, not after being the hand of Providence in Mr. Embleton's accident. We'll just have to wait till Mother comes."

I was tempted to tell Eubie what Mother had said to me the night before but that conversation had been woman to woman. Maybe she thought Eubie was too young to understand. I think she knew he didn't like Mr. Herbert. Lots of times when he came calling Eubie would disappear over the back fence, while I had to sit in the parlor on a hard chair with my hands folded as if

I was waiting for somebody to plunk a bunch of pansies in them.

I could tell that Mother didn't much want to marry Mr. Herbert. Of course, it would be different if she loved him, but if she did she would have told him Yes right off.

I fixed Eubie and me some bread and butter with cocoa on it and went to sit in the front porch swing to wait for Mother.

When she came, she was carrying her wide-brim, navy-blue straw sailor hat in one hand, letting the wind tousle her hair. One look at her face told me the bad news. She came up onto the porch, sat down beside me, and said, "Mr. Wallace says a man should be the one who takes the library books to the mountains. He said if he sent a woman, he'd feel responsible for her welfare."

There went the mountains!

Still being hopeful, I asked, "Did he offer you some other job in the library when you graduate?"

"No."

"What does he expect you to do?"

She squeezed my hand. "Fayette, his only responsibility was to educate me as a librarian in his library school. I paid for that training. He does not have to give me a job in his library."

Thinking of the Hillmans and Cape Cod, I asked her, "What'll we do this summer?"

"I suspect I will spend it writing letters to librarians in other towns asking if they want to hire me. My classmates will be doing that, you know."

I didn't add that instead, she might spend the summer

getting ready to marry Mr. Herbert. I asked, "What if you can't get a job at all?"

She knew exactly what I had in mind. I saw her look down the street to its very end, where Mr. Herbert's law office was located. Then she looked away, her jaw tight, got up, and went through the front door into the house.

I swung slowly in the porch swing, thinking. And as I saw Mr. Wallace's Ford drive by, I got an idea. Carrying it out would take some grit on my part, and I'd have to be careful that nobody ever found out. One good thing, though, I wouldn't be telling more lies. They would be truths, terrible truths.

The next afternoon after school I went down the long, dim hallway to the room I'd been in the year before, Mrs. Wallace's seventh-grade classroom. She was in there, grading papers. I saw her look up at me as I stood in her doorway.

She took off her spectacles, smiled, and said, "Why, hello, Fayette. What brings you here? Come in."

I went in and sat down in the front row desk I had last year and came right to the point. "I need to talk to you woman to woman, Mrs. Wallace."

"Oh, do you? About what?"

I stared at her, such a pretty lady in an ecru frock with a lace bertha. What had made her marry bushy-headed Mr. Wallace from the library? I said, "I need to talk to you about your husband and my mother."

This answer got her interest. I saw her eyes widen but she didn't say anything, so I went on. "And I nee to talk about Mr. Edward Herbert and old Mr. Eml

21

ton too, the men in my mother's life since my father passed away."

She had a queer look on her face. Then she frowned. Her expression made me think I'd better get to the point faster. "Mr. Herbert, who used to be my father's law partner, is pressing Mother to marry him. He knows we haven't got much money anymore, and he does, so he's trying to buy her love. And your husband is maybe forcing her to marry Mr. Herbert."

"What's that?"

At last, she had stopped frowning. "You bet your husband is. When Mr. Embleton fell off the ladder, he lost the person he meant to send up to Big Tree Junction with the library books. I know all about the letter the mountain ladies sent to the sheriff asking for books. My mother, who needs a job in the worst way, volunteered to take the books yesterday, but your husband turned her down. So now she won't have a job when she graduates from his library school, and maybe she won't be able to get a job in this state at all. Even if she does get one in some other town in California, we'll have to sell our house and leave. If she can't find work anywhere, I suppose she'll marry Mr. Herbert. She won't like that and I won't like that and neither will my brother. We'll all be unhappy because of your husband."

"My word, Fayette!" Mrs. Wallace looked astonished.

I nodded at her. "Yes, ma'am. One word Yes from your husband would give Mother a job. It isn't as if she ̄ouldn't do it. She's strong. She used to play tennis. She's ̄t as old as you are. I hear that there'll be a mule driver along, so it isn't as if she'd have to do all the work alone up in the mountains."

Mrs. Wallace hesitated, then said, "But your mother is a woman, and she will be traveling alone for weeks with a strange man. Remember that."

I held up a finger. "No, she won't ever be alone! It's summer, so Eubie and I can go with her It isn't as if we'd get paid by the library. They'll get us for free. It'll work out all right for everybody. Mother will get the books to Big Tree Junction just fine." I didn't add that then she would have time to decide if she wanted Mr. Herbert, and I wouldn't be making a fool of myself in front of the Hillman twins.

"Well, Fayette. I just don't know." She leaned back in her chair and stared hard at the blackboard on the rear wall of her classroom, so I turned around to look at it too. On it was a test about the amendments to the United States Constitution. They reminded me of what she'd said to our class last year, that she thought the next amendment should be the one giving the vote to women. Mrs. Wallace was a suffragette and marched in suffragette parades in San Francisco, dressed all in white with a purple sash over her chest.

I said, "Women can do lots of things people won't give them the chance to try."

"Yes, women surely can." Suddenly she looked straight at me. "All right, Fayette. I take it you want me to speak to my husband in your mother's behalf?"

"Yes, ma'am, I do."

Once more she looked past my head to the blackboard, muttering, "There is the matter of Mr. Murfree

23

to consider, the gentleman with the horses and mules whom the library hired."

"What's wrong with him?"

"He expects to take a man to Big Tree Junction."

"Well, why can't Mr. Murfree change his plans and take a lady?"

Mrs. Wallace put on her spectacles again, looked at me and said, "All right. I'll see what can be done for your mother. I'll speak to my husband tonight."

"Thanks a lot. May I ask you a question?"

"I don't know if I'll welcome it or not at this point, but I believe you plan to ask it in any event."

"Yes, ma'am. As a teacher, do you ever feel like shrieking at the end of the year?"

Now she threw back her head and laughed. "Has it ever occurred to you, Fayette, that teachers look forward to summer vacations as much as their pupils do?"

"Do they?" I thought I'd better get out of there before I messed matters up. "Grown-ups seem to have a lot of troubles, don't they?" I said. "I guess it isn't all that nifty to be grown-up, huh?"

"No, it's not always easy. Responsibility seldom is."

I said, "Thanks again. I'll let you get back to the papers you were grading." And I left her room, being careful not to slam her door behind me, something she hated.

I stood for a moment with my back to it, feeling the grit draining out of me now that I'd asked for her help. Would she keep her word? Could she help Mother?

I was halfway down the hall when I recalled what else I had to say. I ran back to her room, opened her door, stuck my head in, and said, "Please, don't tell your husband that I asked you to help Mother. Please don't mention Mr. Herbert either. Please make your husband think it was your idea."

She glared at me "Don't worry, Fayette. I figured that out all by myself."

"Thanks once more. For a teacher you're really classy, you know." Carefully I shut her door and very quietly ran down the hall and outside into the late May sunshine.

I didn't get to see Mrs. Wallace to ask her how things went the next morning, because I was Miss Uffelman's classroom monitor for all of May and had to be at school to put textbooks on every desk before classes started. I was going to go during recess, but then Miss Uffelman sent me to the principal's office to get something for her. At noon, I got foiled again because Mrs. Wallace had already gone into the teacher's lunchroom, where students were not permitted.

I didn't hang around outside it. Instead, I went to the library, hoping I could see Mother for a minute. I was in luck. There she sat at the circulation desk, stamping due dates on books for an old lady patron and writing up the cards to slip into the old lady's pile of books. I waited for everyone in line to be taken care of. Had Mother talked to Mr. Wallace or not?

Finally she looked up, spotted me staring at her, and by the smile that came over her face I had my answer. Good news! Mr. Wallace had talked with her, and she had got the job. She pointed to the sign on the desk in front of her that said *Quiet* and made a circle with her thumb and index finger. She had the job all right! I'd done it for her, me and Mrs. Wallace. We were all saved. We were all going to Big Tree Junction!

I sat happily in the porch swing that afternoon, waiting for Mother, but when she got home, she didn't sit down with us. She went inside, laughing, and shook her head as she told us, "It was very odd how I got the job. Just after I arrived at the library this morning, Mr. Wallace called me into his office and said he was willing to send me up to Big Tree Junction after all. He said it might be nice for me to take my children with me as companions. Somehow he seemed to know about the two of you, though I have not talked about you at the library. He said he felt your company would be a good thing inasmuch as without you I would be traveling with a strange man. The library trustees would never permit a female librarian to do that."

I said, "They're absolutely right, Mother." I tried to sound innocent. "I'm sure glad Mr. Wallace has heard about us from somebody and thinks we ought to go, too."

"When do we leave?" asked Eubie.

"As soon as your school and mine are out for the summer." She took a deep breath. "There's a lot to do, though, before then. Mr. Wallace will arrange for the saddlebags and choose the books to go. He told me to buy what I will need at library expense, but I am to pay for your food and clothing and for Eubie's tent."

"What'll we have to bring?" asked Eubie happily.

"Two tents, bedding, breeches and boots, that sort of

26

outdoor thing. Mr. Wallace said Mr. Murfree will be responsible for the cooking and setting up camp. I am to set up the library outposts and deal with library matters in general."

I asked, "Outposts?"

"Yes." She sat down and so did we. She leaned forward in her chair, clasping her arms about her knees. "Let me tell you how this is to work. I am to take loads of books on pack mules. Other animals will carry our camping gear and be our mounts. We are to travel from place to place in the hills on our way up to Big Tree Junction, leaving books with mountain people willing to function as future library outposts. We shall take the Monterey library to as many places besides Big Tree Junction as we can find. On our return trip, we will retrieve the books we've loaned out along the way." Mother looked pleased at the prospect.

"In the future, the library will send books by the U.S. mails to the people who will be our library outposts. They will circulate the books, pack them when they are returned, and send them to us by mail. We will send new books back to them. So I am to set up a library network of outposts. Call them branch libraries, if you wish. This mission is much more than simply comforting the ladies of Big Tree Junction with some new books to read." She flung her arms wide. "It will be a big challenge to me, to set up something long-lasting and important in my very first job. How wonderful!"

Suddenly she frowned at us. "Mr. Wallace didn't sound eager to send me, you know. He warned me twice that it would not be easy for a woman and that Mr. Murfree had signed a contract to accompany Mr. Embleton, not a woman and children, into the wilderness."

I snorted and said, "What wilderness? This is California, and it's 1916 not 1850."

Eubie said happily, "Maybe we'll see some wild animals."

To stop his possibly upsetting Mother, I said, "I bet Mr. Murfree could take care of anything that pestered us."

"All right, children"—Mother spoke briskly now—"tomorrow is Saturday. We'll go to the stores that outfit campers, and Sunday when I see Mr. Herbert, I will tell him about my position with the library."

I asked her, "If you do all right on this job, will the library hire you to stay here in Monterey?"

"Oh, Fayette, I have no idea. But Mr. Wallace did tell me today that Mr. Embleton was so shaken by his accident that he has decided not to come back to his job but to move to San Francisco with his sister permanently. There'll be a vacancy in the library, but I don't know who will get the post."

I only nodded. I was hoping that if she did well up in the mountains she could have that job.

The next morning we all went to the dry-goods store, where we got outfitted for the trip with twill breeches, flannel shirts, men's felt hats, yellow rain slickers, and leather low-heeled boots that laced up the front. They weren't cowboy boots, because Mother said you could not hike in high cowboy heels. I tried on my cowboy duds and looked at myself in the store mirror, while Mother bought two canvas tents, three sleeping bags, and some blankets. I wasn't classy looking, but I did appear to mean business if I tucked my long hair up under my hat and scowled. I thought I looked a bit like the brave soldiers who were fighting Mexican bandits on the Mexican border with General Pershing.

Eubie had let me in on a secret of his. He was taking Father's Spanish-American War souvenir trumpet with him. He wanted to blow it when we came into Big Tree Junction to let the "desperate ladies" know the library had arrived.

When Mr. Herbert arrived the next day in his Reo automobile to take Mother for a drive to Carmel, I perched on the stool just inside the kitchen door. It was a good place to hear whatever was said in the parlor, and if Mother had any trouble with Mr. Herbert proposing again, I could come rushing in with a napkin around my finger saying I'd cut myself peeling potatoes. To keep him from pressing her, I'd even nick my finger so he could see real blood, but I hoped I wouldn't have to go that far.

As it turned out, I didn't. He came to our house in the black suit he always wore, with steel-rimmed spectacles and hair parted down the middle, but he stayed only a couple of minutes and then left, driving off in a big hurry.

Mother had met him at the front door in her traveling outfit, and, of course, he asked her right off why she was dressed up like a male engineer or surveyor to go to a classy place like Carmel.

She said, "Edward, I want you to see what I will be wearing when I take the books for the library up into the mountains to Big Tree Junction."

I heard him ask, "To Big Tree Junction. *You*, Lettie?" He didn't sound pleased.

"Yes, me. The library is sending me up there with a muleteer and mules loaded with books."

"With a mule skinner? A man? You'll be traveling *alone* with some man?"

"Yes, with the man Mr. Wallace has hired." Mother's voice was very firm. "Fayette and Eubie will be with us too."

"Lettie, Mr. Wallace ought to be dismissed for his lack of judgment. Sending a female up there is wrong enough. But sending children of a tender age compounds the crime!"

Me, tender? At thirteen? I stifled a laugh.

"Why is that wrong, Edward?"

"Because the mountains south of Monterey are an absolute wilderness. I've defended a number of men in court who came from there. They were half savages. No, I simply will not permit you to go up there. My wife-to-be is not to be tramping around the hills with my future stepchildren, not even if she's being sent by the public library!"

I held my breath, hoping Mother would say what I would have told him. She did. "But, Edward, I am not as yet promised to you in marriage. We will be leaving as soon as school is out."

That was it! She'd said it. Good for her!

He replied, "All right, Lettie. Go! Have it your way. I surely won't keep you from leaving if you tell me I have no right to do so. I will see you when you come back and while you are away, I will hold a good thought for the safety of all of you. I do believe that you and I would be wise while we are apart to consider carefully any plans we have concerning our possible future together."

When Mother didn't say anything further, Mr. Herbert ended the conversation quickly. "Good-bye then, Lettie. I'll show myself out. I imagine you don't want to go to Carmel dressed like a working man. I hope you are still mistress enough of yourself not to want to make a spectacle of yourself there, so I certainly will not insist that you go with me!"

Out he went, shutting the door and front gate hard behind him. Then I heard him crank his Reo and drive off.

The scene was just exactly as I'd thought it would be. Not once had he told Mother that he loved her or worshipped the ground she walked on. I'd seen enough Mary Pickford movies to expect that sort of talk from any man courting a lady. After all, I could read the words "I love you" in subtitles as well as any grown-up could. I was almost certain he hadn't kissed her either.

I came out of the kitchen and asked, "Oh, has Mr. Herbert gone already?"

Mother was sitting on the sofa, looking down at the

31

mouth. She said, "Yes, he's against my taking the job. Fayette, maybe I'm making an error in going to the mountains against his wishes. He is a very intelligent man."

"You aren't making a mistake." I came to sit beside her and put my arm around her. "You can do the job, and if you want to marry some man someday, even him, you won't have to marry to be supported. You'll be independent."

"Yes, Fayette, yes." After a moment, she rose and went upstairs, leaving me to sit alone.

I saw a dark cloud rise in my mind. Though I tried to blow it away, it wouldn't go. Mr. Embleton hadn't wanted to go to Big Tree Junction. Neither had Mr. Wallace, and he had not wanted to send Mother there. Mr. Herbert might know a thing or two after all about where we were headed. I thought I understood enough lawyer talk from hearing my father speak to know that a person who was "defended" in court had done something against the law.

The way I saw it, no matter what might happen in the mountains, Mother just had to make a a good showing for the library. Those books had to get through to Big Tree Junction! And I would do whatever I could to help her.

2

I had no trouble telling the big-eyed Hillmans that we were very nobly giving up our Canadian Rockies trip for something that was fairly close to Monterey. They didn't let out a peep about Cape Cod or their rich old grandmother while I spoke about Mother's very important job and about our traveling on horses to the mountains. Horses were more romantic than dirty old trains any day.

That week ended with me getting graduated out of the eighth grade, Eubie getting passed into the sixth, and Mother getting graduated from library school.

The staff of the library school gave an ice-cream social party for the graduating librarians, but their families were not included. I didn't mind, in spite of missing the ice cream, because I didn't want to see Mrs. Wallace right now. I'd put a thank-you note in her box but that was all I intended to do about her right now.

That night Mother came home with a diploma that proved she was a "real-life" librarian. Now she could show patrons where the encyclopedias and dictionaries were and find answers for questions phoned in over the telephone, not just stamp books in and out and shelve them the way clerks did. She was quite thrilled to be a librarian, and so she should be. Furthermore, she was the only one of the six ladies graduating to have a job.

That night she said, shaking her head, "Fayette, I'm not ungrateful, but it doesn't seem right somehow that I have a job when the others don't."

I said, "Oh, it was the hand of Providence again. If I hadn't asked Mr. Embleton for the book, you probably wouldn't have one either."

"Yes, but it does seem odd that my daughter's request for a certain book caused his accident, and I get the job he was to have undertaken. I told Mrs. Wallace tonight that I felt guilty, and she said that Mr. Embleton's fall was in no way my fault."

So Mother had talked to Mrs. Wallace. Did Mrs. Wallace maybe think I'd pushed Mr. Embleton's ladder? I took a deep breath and asked, "Mother, what else did she have to say?"

Mother shrugged. "Only that she remembered you well from having you in her class last year. Mostly she talked about my going to the mountains. Oh, well, we are definitely going. The library is sending the Overland car at seven tomorrow morning to pick up our personal things. All of the library books have been chosen and delivered to Mr. Murfree to be packed into the saddlebags. We are to be at the livery stable where he boards his horses and mules at seven-fifteen. From there we head directly up into the mountains."

Horses! Mountains! Eubie's eyes had gone glassy with pleasure, and I suspected mine had too.

Mother seemed to be acting sort of odd, however, so I asked, "Aren't you glad we're going?"

"Why, of course, I am, Fayette. What makes you think I would not be? I need this job, don't I? Now I have to go see about more packing." And she went out of the room, going toward the stairs.

Because I was concerned about her, I went up too. As I walked to my room, I took a peek into hers and saw Mother standing in front of her long mirror, wearing her man's felt hat. It looked odd with her yellow-lace graduation frock. She was looking very solemnly at herself. Suddenly she made a funny little frowning face at her reflection, took off the hat, and threw it onto the bed. What a queer thing to do! But she had to be all right, because she shrugged and softly chuckled, then flung her arms wide.

The library Overland was at the door right on the dot, and it found us "booted, and ready to ride," according to Mother, who had not been on a horse since she'd left her Kansas hometown. Eubie and I had never ridden horses, but our father had been one of President Teddy Roosevelt's Rough Riders in the Spanish-American War, so I was sure we'd get the hang of horseback riding fast since it ought to be in our blood.

We piled into the car behind Mr. Wallace, who was driving, with our valises and sat down. I saw how he eyed Eubie's souvenir trumpet, slung over his shoulder, but he didn't say anything about it. I did. "My brother's going to blow it when we come into Big Tree Junction with the books," I told him.

Eubie added, "I'll blow it at any wild animals we see too. It's good and loud, and I've got lots of wind for it."

Mr. Wallace said, "That will be most interesting, I'm sure." He put the Overland into gear and started off with Mother beside him, talking about the news of the Great War in Europe as if he'd been reminded of it by the trumpet. I heard him say, "Mrs. Ashmore, I very much doubt if you'll hear of the war in the mountains at all. When I was there years ago, the Spanish-American War was going on, but I never heard a word about it. When the mountaineers spoke of war, they meant the Civil War. They don't get the news of the world much, and when they do, it's old news."

Mother's reply made me proud. "Well, Mr. Wallace, I shall tell them what I know of the European conflict, what countries are fighting and why."

His tone was heavy. "Don't be surprised if you find that they don't take a lot of interest. Mrs. Ashmore, I have tried to tell you that these people are not like those you have known in Sacramento and here in Monterey."

I couldn't help but ask him, "Then are they like the people in *Heidi*?" Would he even know *Heidi*?

He answered me shortly, "No, they are not Swiss."

Mother exclaimed, "But if the ladies of Big Tree Junction wrote you for books, they must take an interest in things! They must be readers."

"Mrs. Ashmore, those few ladies read. But you won't find hundreds of eager readers in the mountains any more than you'd find them anywhere else. You know what an uphill struggle it is to create readers anywhere. Library school should have taught you that."

Mother said nothing as we went through just-awakening Monterey, but as we pulled up before the livery stable on the edge of town, Mr. Wallace repeated, "Yes, sir, bringing books and readers together is an uphill struggle anywhere at any time!"

Then he got out of the Overland, went around, and held the door open for Mother. Eubie and I got out by ourselves. We stood with Mother while Mr. Wallace walked into the open door of the livery stable, calling out, "Mr. Murfree, the library people are here."

We waited and waited, and after a while a man came shuffling out of the big dim building where horses stood in stalls at the rear wall. He was a stooped-over little man with a rubbery face, gray hair, and a drooping gray mustache. He had on a leather vest, leather pants, a red flannel shirt, black heavy boots, and an old, faded blue cap with a black visor.

He was chewing tobacco and spat a stream of it to one side before he said in a rusty-sounding voice, "I'm here, Denver Murfree is here. I was out at the corral with my animals. At first, I thought you was more riding academy folks comin' after horses, so I didn't come out right off. I don't take to such folks."

"Yes, yes," Mr. Wallace spoke sharply, and pointed to Mother, Eubie, and me. "This is the librarian and her children. They are the people who will go with you to Big Tree Junction."

Mr. Murfree's eyes were crinkled up, so I couldn't see their color, but he didn't take them off us as he said, "A woman in britches ain't a natural sight. I was expectin' three men to go with me, after you let me know I'd need three critters saddled. All right, I'll take 'em, so long as I get the pay you was to give me and so long as this here female and these kids don't get in the way of me and my animals. I signed a paper with you to take somebody up to Big Tree Junction and back, and I sure thought it would be some he's, not a her and two little squirts of him's, and one I see with a cussed blow horn."

Two *him's*? He thought I was a boy. I said, "I'm not a him! I'm a her, and it's a bugle, not a blow horn."

"Aw-right, two her's and a him. That's worse than two him's."

Mother said quickly, "Mr. Murfree, I'm Mrs. Ashmore, Mr. Wallace's librarian. My daughter is named Fayette. My son is Eubie. The bugle is his."

"Aw-right, but he better not blow it. Noah used to be in the Army. There ain't no tellin' how he'll take to hearin' a bugle again."

"Noah?" asked Mother.

"Noah, my oldest mule. He's some years older than the other pack mules, Ham, Shem, and Japheth."

I understood, of course. Noah of Noah's ark and his three sons. I said, "The other mules are Noah's sons, huh?"

Mr. Murfree gazed at me, then began to laugh. "Mules do not have little mules, girlie. You sure don't know much, do you?"

Mr. Wallace interrupted. "Well, I guess everything is in readiness here, and you'll be wanting to get started right away, Mr. Murfree. Do you have the animals packed?"

"Yep, ready to go, except for these here three valises these folks have with 'em. All they got to do is carry 'em around the rear of the buildin' to the corral." Then

Murfree turned around and hobbled off into the darkness of the livery stable.

"Good-bye and good luck, Mrs. Ashmore," Mr. Wallace said, as Mother stood looking after Mr. Murfree with a queer look on her face. I could guess what she was thinking. Murfree wasn't what I had expected either, but then I'd never met a muleteer before in my whole life.

Mother turned to speak to Mr. Wallace, who was headed for the Overland. He'd left its motor running when we got out of it. "Thank you," she said. "I'll try to do the best job I can for the library!"

He said, "Yes, I know you will. Remember now what I told you last night after the graduation ceremonies. There is a U.S. mail service where you are going, and there are telegraph lines here and there in the hills. In case you have any insurmountable troubles, you can wire the sheriff and the library, and I'll see what I can do for you through the sheriff's office."

"Yes, I'll remember! Good-bye."

Suddenly Mother grabbed up her valise and started around the stable. An instant later Mr. Wallace was in his car and rattling away down the road to Monterey.

"Come on, Eubie," I said to my brother, as I grabbed hold of my valise and started off after Mother.

Walking beside me, he asked, "What did you think of old Mr. Murfree?"

"I don't know, but I don't think he was glad to see us. Maybe he had his heart set on Mr. Embleton. Mr. Murfree looks like he wouldn't mind giving us trouble. I know Mother is supposed to be the boss on the trip, but

Mr. Murfree's already given us an order—for you not to blow your bugle."

"I heard, Fayette."

We rounded the corner of the livery stable and saw Mr. Murfree. He must have gone through a door in the rear of the building, for now he was inside a rickety little corral surrounded by long-legged animals. There were nine of them, eight mules and one horse. I knew mules when I saw them even if I didn't know anything else about them. Four mules had packsaddles on them. Four wore regular riding saddles. The horse had no saddle at all, but on its back was a big pack with our new tents tied on top, and it was harnessed with a halter instead of a bridle. Nobody would be riding that animal.

I sighed as I looked at Murfree's animals. Mules! Sure as shooting, we were going to have to ride mules. What a come-down for us Ashmores! I was glad the Hillman twins weren't here to see me and laugh. Mules were not one bit classy.

The mules looked a lot like horses, but they had bigger, longer, floppier ears and different-looking pale eyes. I stared at the mules with packsaddles on them, the mules that carried the library books. One was smaller than the other three. He was black with gray hairs on his nose. He must be Noah, the oldest one who'd been in the Army, probably in the Spanish-American War, eighteen years ago. So Noah was older than I was.

Eubie and I trailed Mother up to Mr. Murfree, who stood a distance away from the mules. The mules were not looking at us, though the white horse was.

Murfree ordered, "Set your duds down on the

ground. I don't suppose you'd be knowin' how to load a horse or a mule?"

What would Mother say to that? "Mr. Murfree, I see we are to ride mules!" she replied. "I had expected you to have horses for us, but no mind. The packing of the animals is not part of my duty for the library system. It is your duty as the muleteer. I am only to deal with matters concerning the lending of the books. We'd better settle the division of the duties right here and now. So please put our valises onto some animal and tell us which mules we are to mount."

Mr. Murfree laughed very loudly, then told her, "Bossy, ain't you. Women! A man had best go slow with the squabs, go careful with the broilers, but run like sixty from the hens."

I gasped. He'd called Mother a "hen" and I supposed I was a "squab." Mother didn't say a word, just dropped her valise and pointed to it. I dropped mine too, and so did Eubie, who was nearest to the mules. The thud woke Noah up. He gave us a wicked look over his shoulder, his ears laid back and his tail twitching.

"Get away from that critter!" bellowed Murfree. He spoke just in time, for Noah suddenly put his head down and kicked backward at Eubie.

"Eubie!" cried Mother.

"I'm okay." He had fallen over and got up wincing, because he had landed on the bugle. It wasn't dented, though.

"Let that be your first lesson about mules, you flat-landers," Murfree said. "I don't think old Noah has took to you." I saw that the man was grinning as he picked up the valises. What a moth-eaten gink he was! He was enjoying Eubie's almost being kicked by a mule.

Mad, I couldn't help but ask, "Mr. Murfree, have you ever been kicked by a mule?"

"You bet, sis. I've got scars all over me to prove it."

"But how many times were you kicked in the head?" I asked.

"Fayette!" cried Mother.

I didn't care how he glared at me. My question did the job, putting the screws to him. It got him moving, tying Mother's valise to the saddle of a chestnut-colored mule.

We stood watching while he tied mine to a black mule and Eubie's to the other chestnut. Then he mounted a sorrel mule, which had a rifle in a holster on its saddle, took hold of the rope at the end of the white horse's halter, rode to the open corral gate, and went through it.

Even if we didn't know what to do, his pack mules did. They watched the white horse pass by, then each and every one, starting with Noah, formed into a line behind the horse and filed out of the corral.

"Hey, they're leaving without us!" cried Eubie.

"Oh, no, they're not. We're leaving too," cried Mother. "Each one of you get on the animal that has your valise on it. Mount from the left side."

That was easier said than done. I grabbed hold of the black mule's reins and got my foot into the saddle's stirrup, but he kept moving about in a circle. Finally I reached up, grabbed hold of the saddle horn, and plunked down into the saddle. I looked around me and found Mother on top of her mule too, but Eubie still on

42

the ground. The shortest one of us all, he couldn't lift his foot up into the stirrup until he pulled his mule over to the water trough, climbed on its edge, teetered a bit, and finally swarmed aboard the mule.

"Mother, what'll we do now?" I yelled. Riding mules wasn't anything reading *Heidi* had prepared me for.

"We follow the library books! Hurry up. Give your mule a nudge with your boot and follow me."

I did what she told me to. I nudged my black, and we shot out of the corral as if we were escaping an Indian attack. Eubie's mule came streaking behind mine, and Mother's behind his.

I felt like screaming for help and the sheriff as we tore down the road that lay behind the livery stable. Instead, I cussed old Denver Murfree for a bad-natured man and prayed that the mule I was riding was truly following the white horse and not just taking me for a run. I surely hoped we Ashmores were going in the same direction as the library books.

How I hung onto my mule! This trip was starting out hard. First there had been Mr. Embleton's accident. Was I going to be accident number two, falling off this galloping animal? I looked along the road for a soft spot to land on, but didn't see any.

With my black mule in the lead, our three mules galloped until they caught up to the pack mules around a bend down the road. Would they stop or go on past Mr. Murfree?

They stopped! My black mule stopped so fast that I almost fell off and had to slide forward along his neck and grab him around it. From where I was stretched out along my mule's neck, I watched Mother rein in her animal, crying, "Whoa, whoa," which she had been crying all along. He stopped too.

Eubie's mule didn't. It went right on running, passing Mother and me and the four pack mules, to where the horse was walking right behind Mr. Murfree's mule. There it skidded to a stop and began to walk beside the horse.

After I slid back along my mule's neck into the saddle again, I looked ahead once more at Eubie, who still rode beside the white horse.

Mother shouted, "Eubie, come back here to us!"

"I can't!" he yelled in return. "This mule won't turn around." I could see how my brother was moving his arms and shoulders, struggling with the reins.

Mother called out to him, "All right, Eubie. Don't try to turn your mule around. Just make him stop where he is until we catch up to you."

I watched Eubie's back straining as he pulled on the bit, but his mule kept right on going.

For the first time, Mr. Murfree took some notice of what was happening to us Ashmores, though he must have heard us galloping up behind him, yelling at the mules. He turned around in the saddle and shouted at us, "That's where Ish wants to be, next to his ma. He always walks beside old Hagar."

I looked at Mother and saw she was biting her lips. She told me quietly, "I think that our muleteer has just told us the name of Eubie's mule, Ishmael. The white horse must be Hagar. Hagar and Ishmael are mother

44

and son in the Old Testament. Well, we know some of the animal's names, but I wonder what our mules are called." She lifted her voice. "Mr. Murfree, what are the names of the other mules?"

"Blackie and Brownie are yours. Mine's named Bruno."

I looked at my mule, the black one. He was Blackie, and Mother's was Brownie. Nobody could ever say that Mr. Murfree was a poet with names even if somewhere in his life he must have gone to Sunday school, though that didn't seem likely somehow.

As Mother and I trailed the other mules, I said to her, "Mr. Murfree doesn't seem to like us, does he?"

"No, he doesn't," she told me tightly. "He feels he's been fooled. He is within his rights. He expected men; he should have been told that a woman and her children were coming. Mr. Wallace should have told him about the change in plans." She let out her breath in exasperation. "But if Mr. Wallace had told him, Murfree might have refused the job in spite of the contract he'd signed with the library. Mr. Wallace gave me a certified copy of it, so I know what was agreed to. Well, what is done is done, I guess. Mr. Murfree and I will have to make the best of it."

"Mother, there's three of us and only one of him. We've got him outnumbered."

"Yes, Fayette, but he knows how to handle the animals and we don't. He knows the mountains and we don't. I do wish you had not said what you did about a mule kicking him in the head."

By now I was sorry about the remark too. It had popped out of me. "I won't talk to him at all then," I said.

"That might be the wisest thing to do until we get to know him better. I'll warn Eubie not to cross him either."

I asked, "Mother, do you suppose these five ladies up in Big Tree Junction have any idea of all the trouble the library's going to?"

"Probably not, Fayette. Library patrons seldom guess what goes on behind the scenes in libraries."

I sighed very deeply and Blackie danced sideways, because he probably wasn't used to ladies' sighs. Yes, this whole business had been a lot of trouble, more than Mother knew. I'd put real mental muscle into it, and I sure couldn't say it had started out very well. I had a hunch that Mr. Murfree intended to get us all to Big Tree Junction, but he would make sure that we didn't enjoy the trip. Mother would earn her pay, all right.

As we wound through Monterey toward the mountains, I thought of what I'd done getting her the library job. Maybe I'd been hasty in arranging things with Mrs. Wallace after all.

Well, time would tell that. I sighed again.

On and on we went, leaving Monterey behind us
going south, passing through Carmel where folks stared
at us either because they didn't see mule trains very
often or they didn't often see mule-riding ladies in
breeches and painful sights like Mr. Murfree.

I'd hoped he'd stop so we could eat lunch at a café but
not him. He only let us pause long enough to water the
animals at a horse trough while we were still mounted. I
was scared to get off my mule in case I couldn't get back
on him.

I learned more about mules in Carmel. The mare behaved well and so did the other mules, except for Noah,
who tried to nip Ham and got slightly kicked in return.
At that point, Mr. Murfree yelled, "You critters stop
havin' fun on the job!" Dismounting, he went to each of
them, pulled down an ear, and said something into it.
Afterward they behaved themselves.

I noticed that Eubie, who was closest to the two fighting mules, leaned toward Mr. Murfree to listen, hoping,
no doubt, to hear what he said to the mules.

Murfree didn't ask the way of anyone in Carmel.
Without hesitation, he took a dirt road that went toward

tree-covered hills to the south. Before long, we had ridden into the trees and began to climb along a trail. I soon found out that we didn't go straight up as I'd expected. We climbed for a while, then followed along level ground, then climbed some more. We zigzagged a lot, but all the same when I looked behind me, I could see that we were getting higher and higher.

And I was getting hungrier and hungrier, wondering if all we'd be getting in the way of meals would be supper and breakfast.

Mother must have read my mind, because she turned around in her saddle and said, "I'm sure there are soda crackers or something like that among the provisions on the white horse. We'll fill our pockets before we set out in the mornings from now on. I suppose we should be grateful that our muleteer has put water into our canteens so we won't die of thirst."

I nodded at her. I'd already opened my canteen and drunk some of the water in it.

Next Mother said, "When we camp, I'm going to have a look at the saddlebags on the mules and see if the library books are packed properly to protect their bindings."

There wasn't anything to reply, but I was glad that she wasn't taking Mr. Murfree's unfriendliness to heart and truly meant to be the boss.

Up and up we went, winding in and out of trees. I recognized redwoods, sycamores, and oaks, with here and there a maple. Miss Uffelman liked botany, and for a week she had taught us how to recognize native Cali-

fornia trees. Then we spent more time studying the native animals, learning which ones were dangerous.

From the top of my mule, I didn't see anything to be wary of, only rabbits, screeching crows, and hawks up in the sky over the trail. Sometimes, as the last rider, I'd get scolded by a squirrel on a tree limb, because Noah had brayed loudly or snorted passing by and upset it. Yes, I could see already that that mule was going to be troublesome, and Shem and Japheth too. Clearly they didn't like each other.

It got hot that afternoon, partly because there weren't any ocean breezes and partly because we were climbing higher and getting closer to the sun. My bottom was starting to ache from the riding. I had a queer sort of saddle, one with a hole in the middle; I could see Blackie's spine through it. It was a McClellan Army saddle, Mother told me. Maybe its being open kept the mule cool, but I couldn't see how when I was over the hole.

We climbed and climbed. Late in the afternoon we came to a little clearing with a creek running through it. There was a doe drinking from it, but when she saw us, she leaped the stream and dashed into some trees. I thought she was lots more beautiful than a mule.

Mr. Murfree yelled back to us from his place in the lead, "This is where we'll camp tonight! Get off your critters and set down by the crick so you'll be out of my way."

More insults to us Ashmores! I looked to Mother and saw that she was getting off her mule, so I slid down off

mine and held my hand to my back, watching Eubie dismount too. How I ached! I was stiff as a board. So were Mother and Eubie, and we walked slowly and painfully to the creek.

I looked at the mules we'd ridden, wondering if they would run away now that we were off them. No, they didn't. They'd gone up to the white mare and were clustered lovingly around her. Mr. Murfree's mule went up to her too. Could the mare be the mother of *all* the mules? No, Noah had to be as old as she was, if not older.

We sat on a fallen log and watched Murfree make camp for us. First, he got the bridles and saddles and packs off the animals, hobbled them, and let them drink at the creek and crop the grass of the clearing. Then he started a fire with brushwood from the clearing and put up the two tents. Our new tents were of stiff canvas and not easy to handle, but he didn't ask us for help. Afterward he threw our sleeping bags and valises inside them and began to rummage in a gunny sack that had been on the mare. From it, he brought out canned goods, pots and pans, and tin dishes.

Supper with Mr. Murfree was pretty bad. Except for the coffee, everything was canned—canned corned beef and canned beans and canned peas. The coffee was roasted coffee beans, which he broke up on a stump with a hammer and threw into a graniteware pot to boil. There was cream for it, canned also.

Remembering what I'd said about his being kicked in the head, I kept my promise to be quiet. I ate what he dumped on my plate with my tin fork and drank the cof-

fee after pouring in as much canned milk as possible to disguise its taste.

Finally, when we were through, Mother said, "Mr. Murfree, I wish to see how the library books are packed."

He growled, "They're packed just fine, missus. I done it myself."

"But I need to see them. It is part of my job."

He grumbled, "I don't see why it ought to be. If a man from the library was along with me instead of you and your kids, he wouldn't be so all-fired fussy. I packed 'em good. But suit yourself, missus. Go take a look."

Mother got up, went over to where the big leather saddlebags were thrown down, and unbuckled the straps. I saw her peer into each of the eight bags, rummage about, then buckle the straps again. Something was wrong. I could tell by the set of her jaw as she knelt, looking into one bag after another.

Through with her inspection, she came back to us at the fire. As she passed Mr. Murfree, she gave him a look that should have shriveled him to dust. He caught it, but he only chuckled.

She said, "Mr. Murfree, I see that you have taken over some of the space in the bags for your personal effects."

"What do you mean, missus?"

"Your whiskey bottles. Those bags are to carry library books. Books are the staff of life to people starving for knowledge. You should know that. You must be a Bible reader to give your animals the names they have."

How the old gink laughed at that! He slapped his thighs. "I can't read at all. All I can do is sign my name.

I bought the critters from an old galoot who named 'em, not me. He was a one-time preacher. You got it wrong, missus. Bread's the staff of life, but whiskey's life itself. I only put three bottles into each bag, enough to last me to Big Tree Junction. I'll get some more there for the return trip."

I gasped. He had twenty-four bottles of whiskey!

Mother demanded, "Did you leave some books behind to make room for all your alcohol?"

"No, ma'am. There was room for both the books and the booze."

"The head of the library will hear of this." Mother was trembling, and her fists were clenched. "I'm sure they didn't know what manner of man you are or they would never have hired you," she added.

Her shock made him guffaw. "I was the only mule driver for miles around who knows these hills and was willin' to go up in 'em," he said. "The mountain folks know me. That's another reason why that galoot Wallace hired me." Then he added darkly, "Well, if it suits you to bellyache about me after we get back to Monterey, you go right ahead and do it."

Mother threatened, "I could telegraph from somewhere for the sheriff to come get me and my children."

He nodded. "You could, if you can find a place to telegraph from on your own. It's mighty easy to get lost up here. Nope, you'd do best to forget about my whiskey being in the load if you want to do your job in the hills. I don't do any drinkin' except by night. Speaking of that, it's time right now." He got up and shambled toward the saddlebags.

"Fayette, Eubie!" Mother spoke sharply to us. "Let's go inside our tents."

Mr. Murfree turned around with a bottle in his right hand and held it out. "How about a nip a this to keep out the cold? There ain't no harm in it." And he laughed again.

"No, thank you," cried Mother, as she went into the tent she and I were to share and Eubie into the other.

I saw by our lantern light that she was shuddering with anger. "That man, that dreadful man!" she muttered, as she took the pins out of her long hair to braid it for bed.

"Mother, what'll we do about him?"

As she pulled off her boots, she said, "There isn't anything we can do. I have no real reason to telegraph to Monterey. We need him to get us to Big Tree Junction. I think we'll simply have to grin and bear him. That's what is making me so angry."

"Mother, do you think Mr. Embleton knew Murfree and didn't want to travel with him?"

"It is possible that he did. It is also possible that Mr. Wallace knows Murfree fairly well and figures that my journeying with him will teach me a lesson that this is not the sort of thing a woman librarian should do."

Feeling guilty, I mumbled, "Maybe it'll turn out all right. He said he only drinks at night, not during the daytime."

"That is what he says." Mother sighed. "Well, I intend to watch him. Tomorrow will tell us if he keeps his word about that." By now she was out of her jacket, shirt, breeches, and underwear and into her nightgown.

She lifted her arms to the top of the tent and moaned. "Fayette, I ache in every part. I can't do my night exercises now. It will be all I can do to brush my teeth tonight. Will you please get some water from the creek for me?"

Because I was still dressed, I said, "Sure," and went to the creek with my canteen. On the way, I passed Mr. Murfree, who was sitting up wrapped in a blanket leaning against a saddle, whiskey bottle in hand, staring into the campfire. He didn't say a word to me, and I didn't speak to him as I came and went.

After we'd brushed our teeth, Mother said, "I suppose we might as well put out the lantern and try to sleep. I'm sorry now that I didn't bring one of the library books back with me to read aloud. I saw one there that would suit my mood just fine, a book of short stories by Edgar Allan Poe. It would take my mind off matters."

Poe? I felt queer all of a sudden. "Is it a skinny black book?" I asked.

"Why, yes, it's a thin black book. Do you know it?"

"It was the book that felled old Mr. Embleton. I guess Miss Uffelman took it back to the library without my knowing it. She didn't read to us anymore after she finished 'The Fall of the House of Usher.' "

Something crawled up my back, a feeling that made me shiver. The Poe book was with us! It had been a hoodoo book for Mr. Embleton. Could it be one for us, too? Like the ace of spades or a black cat or walking under a ladder or the number thirteen? Well, I wouldn't add my suspicions to Mother's troubles.

I said, "I'm too tired to listen anyhow, Mother. I'd

fall asleep in the middle of anything you started to read. Please, let's put out the lantern now."

I was awakened the next morning by the white mare shoving her head and withers inside our tent, snuffling at us as if she thought we ought to be up. In spite of my aching arms and legs, I got out of my sleeping bag and told her, "Oh, go away, Hagar. We'll get up, and then you'll have all this stuff packed onto your back again. Go off somewhere and think about that." I was sure in a bad mood.

Mother asked me from inside her sleeping bag, "Is that Eubie you're talking to?" Her voice sounded sleepy.

"No, I was talking to the horse." I felt awful. There had been bugs crawling inside my sleeping bag all night long, making me itch and scratch though they weren't biters. I was pretty sure Heidi never had to sleep on the ground in the Alps. Those were civilized mountains.

Breakfast was unusual, but we had no choice. It consisted of canned spaghetti and canned bacon and more coffee cooked by Mr. Murfree, who didn't look any the worse for the whiskey he'd had the night before. I couldn't tell how much he did have, because the bottle was nowhere to be seen.

When it came to getting the tents down and the animals packed and saddled, Mr. Murfree sure knew his onions. I had to give him credit for that. I watched him and saw that Eubie, who sat beside the creek, did too. Eubie didn't look any more joyful than I felt. He'd been bothered by bugs all night too, and a couple of them had bitten him.

55

I asked, "Did you hear what Mr. Murfree says to his mules to get them to behave? I saw you listening to him yesterday in Carmel."

"All he said was some stuff that you wouldn't be interested in, Fayette. Forget it."

Cuss words then? That's what I figured. Well, I didn't care to hear them.

I dreaded getting back onto Blackie, but Eubie held him by the bridle for me when Mother told him to, and he did the same thing for her. Then he dragged his mule, who didn't want to leave the mare for a moment, over to a tree stump and mounted from the top of it.

So, aching all over, we started off across the clearing and almost at once began to climb some more. Wherever Big Tree Junction was, it had to be way, way up, because soon we were on a slope high above treetops below. Ahead and to the side of us were high brown buttes and still higher green mountains.

One thing comforted me. We wouldn't go hungry today. Mother had spotted some crackers among the food stores, and when Mr. Murfree was busy, she had given Eubie and me a handful to stuff into our pockets.

Eubie had tried to get his mule to ride back with Mother and me, but it had different ideas. It trotted right up to the white horse as we started out. Often there wasn't space on the trail beside the mare, so Eubie's mule had to move in behind her. We made a long string as we went along—Mr. Murfree on Bruno; the white horse; Eubie on Ishmael; Noah, Shem, Ham, and Japheth; Mother on Brownie; and me on Blackie.

After wading through two creeks and seeing some

deer, we came to another clearing in the late afternoon. This one was bigger than yesterday's, and people lived in it. I saw a house made of logs with a shake roof, not a fancy house, but it was strong-looking. I also saw a corral and barn to the left of the house and on the right a vegetable garden. Just in front of the place was a well, and beside it a chopping block with a little pile of stove wood on the ground.

Mr. Murfree didn't cross the clearing and go on. He rode a distance into it, halted, and called out, "Hey, Si, it's me, Denver Murfree! Don't you or Sarah shoot."

Shoot? I froze in the saddle, though my mule kept on going. What kind of people lived here anyhow?

I kept my eyes on the cabin, and after a time a little, gray-haired lady in a blue calico dress came out the front door. She had a rifle in her arms, sighted on Mr. Murfree.

He shouted, "It's me, Sarah Mackenzie! You wouldn't shoot me, would you?"

"I ought to, Denver, but being a God-fearin' woman, I won't. I'll let somebody else do that someday." Yes, she knew him all right. I warmed to her. I saw her lower the rifle and stand aside as another woman came to stand next to her. Tall, gaunt, and dark-haired, she was middle-aged and dressed in a man's blue shirt and bib overalls.

"Is that you, Malindy?" shouted Murfree. "When did you come back home?"

Malindy, whoever she was, didn't say a word but only folded her arms across her chest.

Murfree called, "Where's Silas?"

Sarah replied, "He's out huntin' up some strayed cows. Who you got with you, Denver?"

"Library folks from Monterey. Two her's and a him."

"Library folks. Way up here?" Malindy spoke now. Her voice was deep and sounded surprised. How she stared at us Ashmores!

Murfree rode closer, and so did we. "Can we camp here with you tonight, Sarah?" he asked.

"Sure. Sure you can." Sarah Mackenzie came forward to meet us, smiling. She didn't have many teeth, but she smiled all the same. Sailing past Murfree, she came up to Mother and offered her hand to her.

Mother shook it and said, "I'm Mrs. Lettie Ashmore. I've come here bringing books to the mountain people. I want to set up library service outposts, where people can come to get books that are sent here by mail. There are books in the mules' saddlebags to start the service."

"Land a mercy, a book lady way up here? Did you hear that, Malindy?" Mrs. Mackenzie called over her shoulder. "They've got books with them that we can look at. Have they got pictures in them?"

"Oh, yes, some have pictures," said Mother. "Do you think you would like me to leave some books here for you?"

"That'd be good," said Mrs. Mackenzie. "Malindy can read what the books say if it ain't too hard goin'. I can look at pictures."

"Can't you read either?" asked Mother, who must have been thinking of Mr. Murfree, as I surely was.

"Not enough to speak of, but my girl, Malindy, can

read some. She's had three whole years of book learnin'."

I gaped at the woman who had only gone through the third grade at her age.

Mrs. Mackenzie said, "You'll eat with Malindy and me tonight. Denver will too. I like to be hospitable, especially to womenfolks. We don't have many callers up here. But all we can do is feed you. We ain't got beds for you."

"We have our tents. Thank you anyway, and supper will be greatly appreciated," Mother said politely.

After Malindy went into the house, Mrs. Mackenzie called out to Denver Murfree, "Denver, I'd be pleased if you'd chop me some stove wood before you leave here. We have enough to cook some chickens for our supper, but that's all. Silas didn't get around to the woodpile before he left after the cows."

"All right, Sarah. I'll do it later on. Say, does Malindy bear me any ill will because of what happened?"

"No, Denver, she figgered afterward that she was better off married to somebody else. She's a widow woman now. That's why she come back home again."

"Oh," was all Murfree said.

"Oh, will do fine, Denver," said Sarah. "Yes, I almost had you as a son-in-law, but I was spared that by your runnin' away from Malindy on the day of the weddin'. Silas and I never held it against you. We figured leavin' the way you did was in your nature."

"It truly was, Sarah. When the preacher came in the front door, I went out the back one."

"It wasn't the back door," Sarah told him. "It was the back window. Now I got to go kill and pluck some chickens if we're to have comp'ny for dinner." Sarah turned on her heel and went away toward the barn, leaving me staring after her. What a very queer conversation this had been. They talked about very private business right in front of pure strangers.

We had a dandy supper of chicken, dumplings, and biscuits that night with the Mackenzie women in their little house. It consisted of one large room, and there were no electric lights; but Mrs. Mackenzie had a pump in her kitchen that she showed with pride to all of us.

We soon found out that Malindy Culpepper, who had once been Malindy Mackenzie, had sold her own mountain farm and come home to her parents after her husband died. Malindy seemed to be shyer than her mother, but I saw right off that she wasn't shy with Mr. Murfree. How she slapped his plate of food down in front of him! I also noticed that he never looked up to glare at her; nor did he say anything smart-alecky. Right after we had some berry pie dessert, he went out the front door and shut it behind him. Malindy did seem to bear him some ill will. I surely would have if any man had done to me what he'd done to her, even if she had been better off married to somebody else.

Once Murfree had gone, Malindy said to her mother, "Nothin's changed, Ma. Denver's gone out for his whiskey."

Mother told her, "Yes, I suppose he has. We found out that he drinks last night."

Malindy said darkly, "If I'd married him thirty years

60

back, I would have been marryin' his bottles, too. I don't want a man who drinks that much." Then she asked Mother, "Are you lookin' for another husband, ma'am, now that you're a widow woman too?"

"Well, no, not actually." I saw that Mother didn't want to talk about Mr. Herbert. Instead, she asked hastily, "Mrs. Mackenzie, will you and Malindy be my outposts here?"

"I guess we might," said Malindy's mother. "We got the time for it. Havin' books would bring folks here to visit us, and I'd like that fine."

"Good, then I'll leave some books with you, and you can spread the word that they are here to be borrowed. All I ask is that you keep track of who takes them and brings them back. On my return trip, I'll pick them up again. Afterward you will get books regularly by mail from Monterey."

"Sure, ma'am, Ma and me will do that," agreed Malindy.

I sat and listened while Mother arranged library business with the Mackenzies. After a time, she started to talk about what Malindy had read; it wasn't much and had been a long time ago. Then Eubie and I talked about motion pictures, something neither of them had ever seen. I told them about movie cowboys; funny men, like Charlie Chaplin; vamps like Theda Bara; and pretty Mary Pickford, who had long golden curls like a little girl. While we talked, I was aware by the outside noises that Mr. Murfree had tackled the chore of chopping firewood.

Mrs. Mackenzie said, "Denver remembered to do his

duty by the woodpile, Malindy. This time I was able to get some work out'a him. By the way he's choppin' away, I'd say he was mad as hops."

Mother asked, "Why does he dislike women so much?"

Malindy laughed and said, "I figgered that out years ago. He was one of nine brothers. His pa and brothers raised him after his ma died when he was born. He knows more about mules than women. He had some mighty odd ideas about things. . . . " She would have gone on telling us interesting things except that moment there came a terrible yell from outside.

Both Mackenzie women jumped up. Mrs. Mackenzie cried, "That's not my Silas lettin' me know he's back with the strayed cows. That's Denver!" She grabbed up the kerosene lamp and headed for the door with big Malindy lumbering after her. Jerking the door open, Mrs. Mackenzie shouted, "Has a grizzly bear got hold of you out there, Denver?"

I heard Malindy say, "No bear in his right mind would have him, he's so whiskey-soaked."

Mother, Eubie, and I hurried outside behind the Mackenzies, and what a dreadful sight we saw. Denver Murfree was dancing around on one foot, holding the other up in the air with blood running out through his sliced boot. An ax was lying beside the chopping block next to an empty whiskey bottle. He'd chopped himself along with the stove wood.

I clapped my hand over my mouth and stood stock still. So did Mother and Eubie but not Mrs. Mackenzie. "Malindy," she ordered, "pick him up and get him inside the house, so I can cut off his boot and see how bad he's hurt hisself. I'll run and get some clean rags for bandages."

We Ashmores watched as Malindy, who seemed to be strong as well as big, lifted Murfree off his one foot and took him into the house. Mother walked around the bloodstained chopping block and picked up the lantern Murfree had been using. As she passed the empty whiskey bottle, she kicked it and it rolled away, clinking against the chopping block.

"Fayette," Mother told me, "and you too, Eubie, come help me look through the saddlebags for a doctor book so we can give Mr. Murfree first aid. Mr. Wallace said that he would put some medical books in with the others."

Mother was certainly keeping her head. She set the lantern on a corral post, and by its light we rummaged through the saddlebags. The first book that came to my hand behind a full bottle of whiskey was a thin one. I hauled it out with a sinking feeling and saw, alas, that it was bound in black leather. I let it slide back down into the bag. It was what I had thought it would be—the book of tales by Poe. That book was a sure-enough pain the way it kept showing up in my life. It was a true hoodoo.

What would we do now that our mule driver had had a bad accident? I knew I should feel sorry about his foot, but I also knew that it would not have happened except for the whiskey he'd drunk. He should have chopped the firewood before he started drinking.

After Mother had gone inside with a first-aid book,

Eubie and I remained beside the corral. The moon came up big and round and pale yellow. By its light, I could see Eubie's face and could tell that he was worried too.

He asked me, "What will Mother do now, Fayette? What if Mr. Murfree can't ride because of his cut foot? Will we have to go back to Monterey? There isn't any place to telegraph for the sheriff to come get us. I looked around. There aren't any telegraph wires here."

"I don't know, Eubie, but I know Mother. I bet you anything she'll want to go on to Big Tree Junction with or without Mr. Murfree." I didn't add that "without" would probably suit her best.

All at once there came a fearful shout from the house that let me know the women were giving Mr. Murfree first aid. He went on howling, and I put my fingers in my ears. A minute later Malindy came running over to the saddlebag that was nearest the house, reached in, grabbed a full bottle of whiskey, and ran back inside. The yelling stopped quite soon afterward.

Eubie and I sat down on the ground in front of the corral. When Hagar came over and shoved her muzzle through the bars, snuffling at us, Eubie reached up to pat her. She couldn't help being the mother of mules. Mother had explained to me that mules had horses for mothers and donkeys for fathers. Because mules were half-and-half animals, they were called hybrids, but they couldn't have mule colts themselves. She'd said that their being hybrids made them stronger than donkeys and less nervous than horses, but I noticed that it didn't seem to make them loving. The white mare was the only one that came over to us now when we were so sad, not any of the mules.

"Horses know things!" Eubie confided to me.

I nodded. Maybe Hagar did know that her master had cut himself. He'd yelled loud enough.

After a while, Mother came out and told us, "Malindy has sewed up his foot. It was a very deep wound and is going to swell, I'm sure. I expect it will be very sore and painful. I know that he won't be able to stand or get his boot on." She sighed. "The Mackenzies agree that he can't ride, much less pack mules and set up a camp. He's passed out now from the pain and from all that whiskey. Malindy poured some on the wound to clean it and the rest of it down him to soothe him."

I said sourly, "That probably leaves only twenty-two and a half bottles, huh, if he had a half bottle before he cut himself?"

"Yes, I suppose so, Fayette." Mother sighed deeply as she leaned on the corral rail and stared at the moon. "Well, it surely creates a big problem for the library and us, doesn't it? I've discussed it with the Mackenzie ladies, who were most helpful. My but they are pleasant people!"

I asked, "How are they helpful? Will they find another driver to go to Big Tree Junction with us?"

Mother looked thoughtful. "The Mackenzie ladies know what the library aims to do up here, of course, and they think it is a splendid idea. I told them that the library has an arrangement with Mr. Murfree that states in the event of his being unable to continue to Big Tree

65

Junction, another driver may complete the journey using Murfree's animals."

I said, "So if they get another driver for us, we're okay?"

"And Mr. Murfree will stay here?" asked Eubie.

"Yes. Mrs. Mackenzie has had experience with accidents and has delivered babies and set broken arms and legs. Malindy has pulled bad teeth and doctored diseases with mountain plants she knows. They say it would be safer to keep him here than try to get him down to Monterey to the hospital. I must take their word for it that he'll be looked after here." Mother smiled faintly. "Looked after, but given no whiskey. Malindy says she'll see to that! Mrs. Mackenzie suggests that we set up our tents ourselves and stay here until her husband comes home. Then he'll go in search of a man called the Possum. The Possum could be our salvation, according to Mrs. Mackenzie. She thinks her husband knows where he may be."

I asked, "The Possum?"

"Yes, he's a person who lives here in the hills."

Eubie asked, "Couldn't Mr. Mackenzie take us to Big Tree Junction?"

"Eubie, I asked Mrs. Mackenzie, and she told me that he doesn't have the touch that mules respect. She thinks the Possum might. I agreed, of course, to hire him if he can do the job. The library will pay him for his services back home in Monterey. Come on, you two, get up. Let's try to get our tents pitched. I think we can do it. I watched Mr. Murfree last night and know where he set the tents down when he got them off the mare."

66

It took some time and a lot of struggling with the canvas, the pegs, and the ropes, but after a while we got the job done. Then, feeling proud, we went inside the tents and slept higher up than we'd ever been before in our whole lives.

Before I went to sleep, though, I asked Mother, "We aren't going back, are we?"

She said in the darkness, "I surely hope not. I just wish I knew more about this Possum individual. Malindy has never set eyes on him. He came to this part of the hills long after she left to marry. Mrs. Mackenzie has only seen him once at a distance. He was up in a tree then, and her husband advised her not to try to talk to him."

"Up in a *tree*, Mother?"

"That's what she said. He was up in a big sycamore, as she recalled."

That information didn't exactly make me feel easy in my mind regarding the man they called the Possum. When I was little, I'd thought living in a tree would be nifty. Now that I was almost grown-up, however, I could see that it would have its drawbacks in rain and cold weather. The Possum must surely be odd if Mrs. Mackenzie was warned not to talk to him. Was he like Mr. Murfree, another one who didn't take to women? Oh, what had I got us into when I'd talked to Mrs. Wallace? Maybe her husband and Mr. Herbert and Mr. Embleton knew more about the mountain people than I'd given them credit for. I'd sure complicated our lives lately.

Mr. Mackenzie came home at breakfast time, driving two black-and-white cows in front of him. He was a small old geezer in striped overalls and an old brown hat that might once have been a derby.

Mother, Eubie, and I were already up and dressed and just about to go into the house for breakfast. Mr. Mackenzie naturally gaped at us, wondering who we were and why we were camped in his yard, but Mrs. Mackenzie came out at once. "Silas," she yelled to him, "I'm sure glad you're back. We got some trouble here. Put them cows in the pasture and shut the gate good on 'em this time. Then wash up, wipe your boots so you don't track dirt inside, and come and eat breakfast with us and the folks visitin' here."

He stopped to shout at her, "Who're these folks, Sarah? Ain't that Denver Murfree's old white mare and mules in our corral? Has he come here agin? Where is he?" His voice got louder. "Oh, Lordy, I forgot Malindy's home! Did she shoot him after all, the way she used to say she'd like to?"

"No, not yet," cried Mrs. Mackenzie, "but he's the trouble all right. He's hurt hisself powerful bad." She waved at us. "These here are library folks from Monterey. Silas, do what I ask you, and I'll tell you everythin' at breakfast. But before you go to the pasture with the cows, tell me if you got any notion where the Possum is nowadays. Did you see him?"

"Nope, but I heard him up on a ridge at daybreak. He was whistlin'. It was the Possum all right."

"Good. You can find him then." Mrs. Mackenzie spoke to us Ashmores. "Come on in and eat. Then I'll send Silas after the Possum."

68

Mother said, "But your husband must be very tired from getting the cows. Won't he be too weary to go up into the hills again?"

"He won't be that weary. He most likely tethered the cows to a tree last night and slept after he rounded them up. He don't like to travel by night with all the cougars and bears around."

I asked her, "How's Mr. Murfree?"

"Restin'. Hurtin', but restin'. Malindy told him that you folks had best go on without him, so you won't have to speak to him. He said you couldn't leave here without a mule driver, because the mules won't move for just anybody who comes along. Malindy said we might get hold of somebody else to work the animals, and he said that would be jake with him if the library female took it on herself to pay him back for any hurt or dead animals."

"Yes, the library would pay him," Mother said, and then she sighed.

Inside we found Malindy sitting on the edge of Mr. and Mrs. Mackenzies' bed, which held a glaring Denver Murfree, covered to the shoulders with a patchwork quilt.

Mother asked him, "How do you feel this morning, Mr. Murfree?"

"How's a man supposed to feel when he's just about chopped off half of his foot and been fed a bowl of cornmeal mush by a cruel-natured female?"

"He should feel sadder but wiser," scolded Malindy, before Mother could reply.

69

Malindy got up off the bed, took the rifle from its rack by the front door, and went out, shutting the door behind her.

Mrs. Mackenzie explained, "Malindy won't be havin' breakfast with us. She and Denver have already et. Now she's got some outside work to do."

Eubie asked, "With a rifle? Is she going hunting?"

"No, just practicin' to keep her aim up."

A moment later Mr. Mackenzie came in. He said, "Hello, Denver," and got no reply. Then he started in with us on the platter of home-cured bacon, scrambled eggs, and biscuits. Mr. Mackenzie didn't seem to be a talkative man while he ate, and, not wanting to annoy him, we Ashmores ate quietly too.

Then all at once we heard the sound of a rifle being fired and immediately after the sound of breaking glass.

"What's that?" cried Mother.

Mrs. Mackenzie announced, "That's Malindy takin' care of Denver's whiskey supply."

Eubie and I jumped out of our chairs and pressed our noses against one of the two small front windows. What I saw made me gasp, then grin. Malindy had set up a long line of whiskey bottles, on top of the fence rail between the corral and the barn, and she was drawing a bead on them with the rifle. *Pop, crash,* there went another bottle hit smack in the middle. I glanced over my shoulder at Mr. Murfree, who had put both of his hands over his face.

On and on the shooting went until there were only two bottles remaining. Didn't Malindy plan to shoot them, too? No, apparently she didn't. I watched her put one of them back into a library saddlebag and, with the rifle under her arm, start back to the house with the other.

As she came inside she set the bottle on the table. "Well, Denver, that's that! It'll be coffee, water, or milk for you till you're ready to get out and around. This bottle here ain't for drinkin'. It's medicine for us. So's the bottle I put back in a bag for the library folks to use."

Mother muttered, "I don't see why we need any whiskey."

"Wait and see. You never know what's around the corner."

"Yes, sir." Silas Mackenzie, who hadn't missed a bite of his breakfast during the shooting, got up. "I ain't promisin' you anything, book lady, but I'll try to fetch back a mule driver for you before the day's over."

After a sip of coffee, Mrs. Mackenzie said, "Good luck, Silas. Tell the Possum he'll be doin' a good deed in the eyes of the Lord in helpin' the library folks. Maybe that'll do the trick and get him back into civilized ways like ours."

Civilized? The Mackenzies were supposed to be civilized? I felt like laughing, but I caught Mother's warning eye and kept quiet. They had been very good to us, and I was ashamed of myself.

Just before we all left the breakfast table, Malindy said something that made me smile. "If we loan out a book to somebody who don't bring it back on time," she declared, "I'll go after it with the rifle."

Mother's answer surprised me. "That's the proper spirit, Mrs. Culpepper. Loan the book out, but do be

71

sure you get it back. You'll have to keep track of the books."

Malindy said, "I can read and figure enough to do that. It'll be all right. But leave mostly books with lots of pictures in 'em for folks who can't read. Those books will be most favored."

I shook my head. People who couldn't read taking out library books? That was something for you.

Mother noticed my head shaking and said, "Fayette, looking at pictures can lead to reading. That's how small children start, you know. A collection of picture books could be a first step to getting people hereabouts to want to read and perhaps in time to setting up a school for adults. Malindy is right."

I didn't say anything more. She was the librarian, not me, but I knew as she sorted out books with lots of pictures in them that she was a plenty worried brand-new librarian.

Mr. Mackenzie came back in the middle of the afternoon, and he wasn't alone. With him was a man who
carried a bedroll tied across one shoulder. He must have
been the biggest and the shaggiest man I'd ever seen in
my life. He had a black beard, long black hair under a
black slouch hat, and dark buttoned-up coat and trou-
sers. When he came closer, I saw that he didn't wear
shoes but had leather tied over his huge feet.

"Great heavens!" Mother said.

I asked her, "Is that the Possum? He looks more like
an ape."

"I imagine he is, Fayette."

Eubie said, "He doesn't look one bit like a possum to
me."

Silas Mackenzie called out, "Sarah, Malindy, come on
out. I got Turlock with me."

At the hail, the two women came out of the house and
stood with us. I noticed how Mother sort of stepped sideways, edging up to big Malindy. I edged up to Mother
and Eubie to me.

The two men stopped in front of us, Mr. Turlock
towering over Mr. Mackenzie by a head and a half. Silas
Mackenzie pointed to his family and said, "Turlock, this

here is my wife, Sarah, and my daughter, Malindy, a widder woman now." Then he pointed to us Ashmores and said, "The lady in britches is the book lady, Missus Ashmore, who's a widder woman too, and these are her two young'uns."

There was silence while everybody looked at Turlock and he looked at all of us; then he looked away over the meadow.

Finally Mother said, "I'm glad to make your acquaintance, Mr. Turlock." She took me by the hand, and we both stepped forward to look up under the man's hat.

I saw his eyes, dark and glowing, stare down at us, then gaze away over our heads at the corral. He said in a very deep voice, "You got mules all right. Mackenzie said you need someone to look after your mules on the way to Big Tree Junction?"

"Yes," said Mother. "They don't belong to me. They belong to a man hurt inside."

Turlock lifted a big hand as if to brush away Mother's explanation, but she went right on. "I am a librarian. There are library books in the mules' saddlebags for people in these mountains."

"You got books about birds and animals?"

"Why, yes, we do."

"If I come with ya, I can look at 'em?"

"Of course, you can. You pay taxes to maintain the public library too."

"I don't pay taxes." His voice got even deeper. "But if I take ya to Big Tree Junction, can I look at yer books anyway?"

"Certainly. And you'll be paid wages, too."

Once more the enormous man looked at Mother. He said, "I ain't askin' to be paid. Mebbe later we'll talk about that. Not now. You can figger out afterward what I'm worth to ya. I ain't got a lot of use for money. I'll go with ya, because it's time for me to go where yer headed." Then he stepped forward, scattering people right and left, as he went toward the corral.

Nobody spoke, and nobody took his or her eyes off the stranger either. I watched him go up to the railing of the corral and lean on it. He was so tall that his back hunched way over. The white mare lifted her head from the feed trough, looked at him, nickered, and stamped her right front foot. She didn't move, but all the mules did. While the mare nickered, they looked at the Possum, stood stock still for a long moment, then wheeled in a body and went to the far end of the corral. There they bunched up together, not nipping or kicking one another, but all of them turning around to eye him.

What an effect this big galoot had on the eight mules!

"Land a mercy, would you look at that?" whispered Mrs. Mackenzie to Mother.

"Yes, I see. Good heavens, he seems to have buffaloed the mules just by looking at them." Mother sure looked astonished, and I was astonished too.

"Do you suppose Mr. Turlock is all right?" Mother asked Mr. Mackenzie very softly. "I mean is he competent?"

"Yep, he's all right. He says he wants to go up to Big Tree Junction now. He can handle your mules for you just fine. He's been a mule skinner before. He told me that he's ready to start right now."

Turlock went on gazing at the mules, who hadn't moved except to press closer to the far railings of their corral.

"Mother," I asked, "do you think he should sign an agreement to go with us?"

Mr. Mackenzie explained, "Turlock says he ain't got no use for papers. He won't do anything that ain't on his own terms. He's danged independent in his way of living. He ain't like old Denver if that's what you folks are scared of. He don't need to sign any papers. Offhand, I'd say that the Possum's word is good enough."

Mother asked, "Mr. Mackenzie, how does he feel about traveling with women?"

Mackenzie took off his hat and scratched his bald head. "Far as I know, he leaves them alone and they leave him alone."

I couldn't help but say, "Given his looks and fame as a tree sitter, I can see why ladies leave him be."

"I just talked to him four times before," Mr. Mackenzie said. "He's only been around this part of the hills for a few years. All of a sudden he showed up here a couple of springs ago. I don't know much about him. I warned my wife to leave him be, but he acts aw right with me."

I looked again at Turlock. Would he rob us after we left here or do worse to us? Mother hadn't brought much cash with her, because we had the library food supplies. The only jewelry she had was her thin gold wedding ring. I didn't have anything at all but a locket, and all Eubie had was his old Spanish-American war trumpet.

Malindy said, "You folks better take this big galoot if

you plan to go on. You won't find anybody else up here."

How Mother was frowning. "Yes, I do plan to go! It's what the library expects of me!"

Eubie added, "And the ladies of Big Tree Junction too."

I didn't say anything, but I vowed to myself that I'd keep a sharp eye out for any telegraph poles along the trails we traveled. There had to be a telegraph office somewhere, so we could send a wire to the sheriff if Mr. Turlock turned out to be troublesome. Suddenly a nickname for him popped into my mind. It was the Terrible Turlock.

I felt sure I'd got the right name for him when he finally turned around and said, "These here mules know who's boss now. They'll behave all right, even that little black one that makes all the trouble and the skinny, lop-eared one at the far end."

I gasped. He was talking about Noah and Shem. "How did you know that old Noah makes trouble?" I asked.

"Because he's got a lot of white in his eye, more'n the others. Come to think on it, you got more white in yer eyes than most girls do. Bold, ain't you? Sassy? You take a lot on yerself, I bet."

I gulped, thinking of my lies to the Hillman twins and my secret talk with Mrs. Wallace. This gink was somebody to be on guard against all right. He'd not only scared the mules by just looking at them, he could be a mind reader, too.

Eubie and I stayed out of the house when Turlock,

Mother, and the Mackenzies went inside. The Possum didn't stay long. He came out, stared at the two of us out of the corner of one black eye, said not a word, and went past the corral and into the little forest behind the pasture. We watched him cross it and disappear into the trees.

Eubie said, "Maybe he didn't take the job after all."

I didn't answer, because just then Mother came out of the house. "Well, it's all been settled. Mr. Turlock will handle our mules. I've had a few private words with him."

I told her, "He's gone away. He went into the woods."

"Yes, he said he wouldn't stick around here, but he promised to be back tomorrow morning. Tonight we'll be guests of the Mackenzies again. They won't take any money from me, though I am offering to pay them for what we eat. Aren't the Mackenzies fine people, and so helpful to the library? I hope we find such mountain friendliness everywhere we go."

I gave Eubie one of my fish-eyed looks. What was wrong with her? Did she think Mr. Turlock was friendly? Well, maybe he'd talked nicer to her inside than he had to us. A hard thought hit me. Maybe he didn't mind being around ladies but didn't like kids. Just looking at him made a person wonder if he'd ever been a kid. I sure hoped Mother was right about this man who'd come out of the forest into our lives and gone right back into the trees.

I didn't say good-bye to Mr. Murfree, nor did Eubie, but Mother stayed behind to do so after a supper of venison stew with the Mackenzies. What a terrible lot of yelling and cussing came from inside their house. Pretty soon Mother came out, holding her hands over her ears.

I asked, "Is that how he said good-bye?"

"No, he grunted good-bye at me. He's yelling at Malindy about shooting his bottles. They'll quiet down soon. I think they are really quite fond of one another, and he regrets having jilted her."

I couldn't understand how any woman could be fond of Mr. Murfree but didn't remark on it. "Does the Possum drink too?" I asked.

As she looked in her little cloth bag for our toothbrushes, Mother said, "You know, I asked about that. Mr. Mackenzie said he is not a boozer, and when I asked Turlock point blank if he 'indulged in whiskey,' he said it was bad for a person. If he isn't telling the truth, he'll find only the one bottle of whiskey, and it is for the mare!"

"For the *horse*, Mother?" exclaimed Eubie.

"Yes, Mr. Murfree told the Mackenzies that Hagar likes a bit of whiskey when she gets weary and cold." Mother sighed as she came up with the toothbrushes in her hand. "Well, I would say that things are settled here. Mrs. Mackenzie and Malindy will maintain the library outpost splendidly. They have the proper spirit. On his hunting expeditions, Mr. Mackenzie will spread the word in this part of the mountains that books are available here."

I nodded. I'd seen the pile of library books stacked up in the Mackenzie house. In fact, I'd added something to them! I'd found the Edgar Allan Poe book in the saddlebag and put it on top of the pile when nobody was looking. I'd feel easier in my mind starting out with the Terrible Turlock if that hoodoo book stayed behind here with the Mackenzies.

Morning came with the sounds of birds and the noises of Noah, the noisiest mule. We all got up, dressed, washed, packed our valises, and then we went into the house to eat a last breakfast. When Mr. Murfree spotted us, he turned over in bed and stuck his face into the pillow.

Mr. Mackenzie, who'd eaten already, stood at the window looking out. As I had my last bite of pancake, he said, "Here comes the Possum over the pasture."

I asked, "Why does he want to go to Big Tree Junction?"

"I dunno. He didn't tell me about his business, and I didn't ask him." He nodded. "You'd do best not to ask him either. Let him tell you what he wants to."

Mother said, "Thank you for the advice. I agree with it. And thank you for all you have done for us on the library's behalf."

Suddenly Malindy got up from the table and said, "That reminds me. Ma and I think maybe you left us too many books for this part of the hills. You won't be gone too long anyhow. So take some of these back and leave them somewheres else. I'll stuff them in the saddlebags for you."

I watched her go over to the stack of books and take

six off the top. To my disgust, I saw Edgar Allan Poe being carried out the front door too. I hadn't got rid of him at all! "The Fall of the House of Usher" was going with the Terrible Turlock.

Watching Malindy leave, I made myself another vow. Somehow I'd get rid of that book at our next stop along the way to Big Tree Junction. I was convinced that it was tied up with the luck of us Ashmores, and we needed good luck, not a hoodoo.

Whatever else he might be, Turlock was good at taking down tents and packing them. He'd camped before all right. He did the work even faster than Murfree had. Mr. Mackenzie had offered to help, but Turlock grunted and said, "No." He refused again when Mackenzie offered to help him pack the mare and saddle the mules.

We all watched the Possum lead the haltered mare out, look her in the eye, pat her neck, then throw the load on her and tie it down. Afterward he loaded pack mule after pack mule, starting with old Noah, with the library's big leather saddlebags. The mules eyed Turlock, their eyes rolling in their long heads, and they trembled a bit, but they didn't kick or bite, not even Noah. They stood good as could be while he got them ready and led them over to join the waiting mare.

Then he told us, "Mount up." When we were ready, he got onto Bruno, the mule Murfree had ridden, and started away without saying a word of farewell to anybody.

"Good-bye, thank you again," Mother called to the Mackenzies, as we started off.

"So long, ma'am," cried Malindy. "Don't ya fret over Denver. I'll see to him for you. He'll be better when you get back here. I've got him now. And don't worry about your library books either. I'll see for sure that they get back here to me on time for you to pick them up."

Eubie's mule trotted right up beside the mare, and I saw Turlock turn his head to watch. He only nodded as if the mule was taking his natural place. Sure as could be, we wouldn't be enjoying Eubie's company on this trip; the white mare would.

I asked Mother, "Aren't you nervous?"

"Yes, of course, Fayette. But I'll try to keep up my courage. You keep yours up too."

"I'll try."

So we climbed some more, up and up, and sometimes we rode along the top of a mountain ridge where we could see great naked brown buttes rise in the distance beyond the forest, which was green as the emeralds in a ring I'd seen in a jewelry store window in Monterey. No, these mountains weren't like Heidi's snow-covered, sharp-pointed Alps. But they were mountains all right! Even blindfolded, I would have known we were high by the way I was breathing hard, trying to get more air into my lungs.

The mules didn't seem to be bothered by the height. They just followed Hagar, who followed Turlock's mule along a path that led through the trees. Sometimes we had to wade through creeks and climb up steep banks, sending a shower of little rocks clattering down behind us. And everywhere we went were screeching squirrels, letting us know that they didn't like our passing by.

Mrs. Mackenzie had kindly put up a lunch of chicken sandwiches for us, and Mother had them in a bag with her. When it was noontime and the sun was straight overhead, she took them out, handed two to me, and asked me to ride on ahead and give one to Eubie and the other to Mr. Turlock.

I dug my heels into my mule, and he trotted forward into the little clearing we were passing through. I came up to Eubie, who took the sandwich and began to stuff it into his face right away. Then I rode up to Turlock and held the second sandwich out to him. I said, "Here, it's a chicken sandwich from Mrs. Mackenzie."

He looked at me out of those dark eyes. "No, I don't eat dead bird."

I pulled up Blackie and stood waiting, still holding the sandwich, until Mother's mule caught up to mine. "He said that chicken is dead bird, and he doesn't eat it."

"All right, Fayette, we'll share it. I guess I'd better not give him one of the hard-boiled eggs either."

"No, he'd say that was dead bird too. I wonder what he *will* eat."

"We'll find out tonight when we camp. I wonder where that is going to be?"

The camping place Turlock chose was another clearing. There was a house, barn, and corral beside it, but this place wasn't like the Mackenzies'. It was a deserted homestead, sad and lonesome, with tall, dark pines that swayed in the afternoon wind behind it.

He reined his mule, got off, and came up to Mother. "I'll set up camp here. Keep out of the old house and barn. They ain't safe."

Mother said, "All right, Mr. Turlock. We have canned food with us, beans, spaghetti, corned beef, canned fruit, coffee and bacon. I trust you'll eat that sort of food?"

"I'll eat it, I guess, if mebbe sometimes you eat what I get out of the woods."

I said, "I like venison."

Without looking in my direction, Turlock said, "I mean green things I might fetch ya. I don't kill deer. I don't kill anything that don't come after me."

Mr. Turlock was quiet for a long time, looking over the tops of our heads, though we were still on our mules and he was on the ground. Then he muttered, "It's been a long time since I had woman-cooked grub. Aw right, I don't see why not."

"Fine, Mr. Turlock. I will cook," said Mother.

"Turlock. Just Turlock will do. I answer to Possum too."

After he left to see to the unpacking, I said to Mother, "The Possum's sure a queer one. Has he always lived up in these mountains?"

"Not always, but I think we had better not pry into his affairs or he might leave us in the lurch up here."

"Mother, maybe we can get somebody else farther along on the way to help us?"

"Perhaps, but perhaps not. We simply cannot risk trouble, Fayette. It would be very easy for us to get lost in the mountains or have some sort of accident alone.

Mrs. Mackenzie told me that the fogs they have here can be extremely heavy. We have to keep out of trouble."

I nodded. We also had to get rid of Edgar Allan Poe. All day I'd been thinking of the hoodoo book in Shem's left saddlebag.

After the animals were hobbled and a fire was started, Mr. Turlock began setting up our tents. Eubie came back to us, and I grabbed hold of him. "How did you get along with that gink?" I asked. "Did he talk to you? What did he tell you?"

"Not much. I did most of the talking. He listens real well." Eubie sat down on a log. "I tried to be polite, so I asked him if he wanted to sleep in my tent in case it rains. He said he hated not seeing the sky, so he'll sleep outside."

"That is his privilege," agreed Mother.

I asked, "Do you suppose he'll climb a tree and stretch out on a limb?" Eubie giggled.

After Mother made the supper, I washed the pots and pans, tin cups, and plates in water from the little spring behind the tumbledown house. I didn't fancy that chore, even at home where I had hot water, and by the time I was through it was getting dark.

Carrying the flour sack with the clean things in it, I had to come down a path on the way back to our camp. Because it was sort of steep, I watched how I walked and went slowly. As I put my feet down with care, I noticed something moving a little distance away under some tall evergreen trees. My heart came up into my mouth, and I froze where I was. Was I seeing a big grizzly bear getting up on his hind legs? No, not a bear. Bears didn't wear hats. It was Mr. Turlock, who had been down on his hands and knees so he looked like a bear. He came toward me on the path and without a word went by me down to the fire.

What had he been doing up here by the spring? I waited until he was out of sight and then went over to where he'd been kneeling. What I saw made my blood run cold—a line of wooden-board grave markers, nine of them in a long row. I bent over to read what was on them. Even though the knife-carved letters were faded by the weather and years of time, I could still make them out.

They started at one end with the name "James" and ended at the other with "Baby Dick." In my heart, I knew that these names had to be the people who had once lived in the abandoned house. The wooden markers all had the same year of death under their names, 1879, and the same month of June.

All nine of them also had the same last name— Turlock!

Had this house been the Possum's boyhood home or the home of some of his relations? What had happened here in 1879? Had Indians killed off a whole family of settlers? Were there still wild and angry Indians in the mountains?

No, there couldn't be, not in 1916; these were modern times. But 1879 wasn't so modern, though. I knew my history. General Custer had got himself and his soldiers killed at the Battle of Little Big Horn just three years earlier.

What had I got us into? I could ask Turlock, but I

was afraid to. Even in the twilight, his scowling face had been terrible as he went by me on the path.

With the dishes, pots, and pans clanking in the sack, I hurried down the path to our campsite, telling myself in a whisper, "Keep your nerve!" I gritted my teeth to keep them from chattering and didn't say anything to anyone about what I'd seen until sometime later, when I went into our tent with Mother and we'd shut the tent flap. Then I told her about the graves and that I'd seen the Possum hunkered down up there.

Her eyes widened in the lantern light, but she said only, "Go ask Eubie to come in here, please."

I untied our flap, went next door to his tent, and called out, "Mother wants you." What did she want him for? I wondered.

He came over to our tent and stood leaning on the one post that held it up till Mother told him to stop. Then she said, "Eubie, I saw that you talked again with Mr. Turlock after supper. Did he tell you anything then about this old homestead?"

Eubie nodded. "Sure. He said it used to be his home when he was around my age. That was a long time ago."

Oh, how he could annoy me. Why hadn't he told us that?

"Is that all he said to you?" asked Mother.

"Uh-huh."

Mother sighed, thought for a moment, then asked, "Eubie, could you please ask him now if he has any living relatives in this part of the hills?"

"Do you want to go visit them, Mother?" asked my dumb brother.

I said, "No, Eubie, we don't!"

Mother said calmly, "We'd just like to know something of his family."

"Okay. I'll ask him." And Eubie left the tent.

I asked Mother, "Do you suppose the Possum will tell him? He might think he's being nosey."

"I don't know, Fayette."

After waiting for what seemed a long and gloomy time, Eubie came back, looking very pale. He sat down on top of my sleeping bag, without asking my permission, and said, "The Possum told me. He said he's the last of the Turlocks. He says the others are all buried behind the house. I didn't go up there because it's dark now. He said he figured you saw the graves, Fayette."

"I sure did. Eubie, what happened to his folks?"

"When he was a kid, he got sent away to help his uncle with some farm work. While he was gone, some bad men his pop had fought with years before came hunting for the Turlocks and killed everybody in the family."

"Oh, my God!" Mother said slowly, letting out her breath. "How terrible! And he was the only one who escaped, simply because he wasn't here at the time?"

"Yes, he said he was lucky. Some folks who lived on the other side of the ridge heard all the shooting and rode over later when it was all over. They buried his folks and carved the markers. When the Possum came to the house, they were all gone, and he was the only Turlock left. He was out on his own when he wasn't much older than I am."

I asked, "Did he go back to the uncle he was working for?"

"No, he didn't like him. He whipped his cousins and him a lot. He says he comes back here sometimes to pay his respects to his family."

"The poor, poor man," said Mother.

I told her, "I'll go tell the Possum how sorry we are about the murderers."

Mother put her hand on my arm. "No, don't do that! Turlock doesn't strike me as the kind of man who likes sympathy. Besides, he told these things to Eubie, not to you."

"How come he favors Eubie so much?"

Eubie answered me, being a smart aleck, "Because I'm a boy and he's a man. What'd you expect?" How uppity Eubie was. "Old Turlock's sitting beside the fire with a library book right now. It's a big, fat, red one."

Mother nodded. "Yes, I know that one. It's about birds and beasts of the world and is full of illustrations. I told him about it and where to find it when he asked for a book on nature."

I asked, "Does he know how to read?"

"He says he does, but I'm not sure," Eubie replied. "He doesn't even know that Woodrow Wilson is our president these days. Where's he been so long?"

I told him, "Up in a tree. You don't get a lot of news up there."

Mother sighed. "Turlock's business is his own. Remember that, please! Mr. Mackenzie warned us to mind our own affairs. Now, Eubie, go back to your tent. Don't pester Turlock about the book. Stay on his good side. One of us has to communicate with him. So far you've made good progress with him. Thank you, you've done well."

Oh, how Eubie puffed out his chest. I was tempted to say something to bring him down to size but thought better of it. Mother wouldn't like us to quarrel up here when she already had plenty of trouble.

I vowed that I would steer clear of the Possum, who didn't like the whites of my eyes. In the future, when I looked his way, I'd squint at him. Maybe I would be smart to squint at everybody in the mountains. There might be some sort of superstition about wide-eyed girls up here. Yes, I was starting to wonder about the folks we might meet over the top of the next big green hill we came to. I knew that Mother was, too.

Our eight mules behaved nicely for Mr. Turlock, better than they had for Mr. Murfree, who owned them. I watched Turlock get them packed and ready to go the next morning, and they didn't give him one bit of trouble again. He talked to each one softly, so softly that I couldn't hear what he said, though I tried. They acted so polite toward one another that I walked up to pat Blackie before I got aboard him. Oh, what a mistake that turned out to be! He gave me a look, laid back his ears, snaked out his head, and aimed for my hand with his long, yellow teeth. I jumped out of the way just in time to keep from being bitten.

"You leave that animal be!" roared Turlock, who was packing Hagar.

Though I was shaking, I called back to defend myself, "I was only going to pet him."

Turlock's voice was quieter. "A mule ain't a pet, sis. It's a workin' animal. Come in on a mule from the side, not the front or back, and don't try to get friendly with him. Don't you know anything about mules?"

This taunt got my goat. "No, neither does my brother, who almost got kicked by his mule! We're town folks. We know about automobiles. Do you?"

He gave me a look from under his heavy eyebrows and said, "Not much. I seen 'em, though. This ain't automobile country. Maybe it will never be and that could be a blessin' in the long run."

I said, "Automobiles are going to put both horses and mules out of business. You ought to see the nice touring car Mr. Herbert, a friend of Mother's in Monterey, owns."

I noticed that Turlock had stopped tightening the ropes on Hagar's load. He stood quietly, then asked, "Herbert, huh? What does he do down in Monterey?"

"He's a lawyer."

"A lawyer, huh?"

"Yes, and a very smart one too. Lawyers are plenty smart. He's one of the smartest in town." Never would I have believed I'd ever brag on Mr. Herbert, but here I was doing so as if I liked him. The mountains were sure having a queer effect on me.

As he continued loading Hagar, Turlock told me, "There's no use living with an argument. I don't plan to give you one." Then he turned his back on me, rude as

could be. "You keep your cars, and I'll stick to animals."
Oh, it was hard to feel sorry for him, even though he was
an orphan.

A half hour later we rode away from the deserted
homestead, and I noticed that, even if it had been his
old home, the Possum didn't glance back once at it. We
went uphill and downhill some more and camped that
night in a little field where wild oats grew beside a
stream. Nobody had much to say at supper, and nothing
happened that night. In the morning when I got up,
though, I found Mr. Turlock doing something that
really surprised me—sewing. He was sitting by the fire
sewing a bridle with twine.

He saw me standing in the opening of our tent, staring at him, and he said, "There was a needle and twine
in a bag that goes on the mare. We had us a visitor last
night who came to chew on your mule's bridle head-
band."

"A visitor who came to *chew*?" asked Eubie, just after
he came out of his tent with his toothbrush in his hand
and a towel over his shoulder to go to the brook.

Turlock nodded and bent to his sewing. "A porcupine was here. It come out of the woods to get the salt it
needed from the mule sweat on the bridle."

As I made a face at the thought of mule sweat, Eubie
asked, "How'd you know it was a porcupine?"

"I saw it leaving."

Eubie asked, "You didn't try to kill it?"

"Why would I do a fool thing like that, boy? Let me
tell you and yer sis something. It's sort of law up here
not to kill a porcupine, because if yer unarmed and

92

starving and on foot, you can't catch anything else but a porcupine. You can kill one of 'em for food with a tree branch. Mountain people who have some manners leave porcupines alone for folks who may have to kill one to go on livin'."

Mother had come out by now. "What interesting information," she said. "I didn't know that."

He grunted. "Not everythin' worth knowin' comes out of books." Then he got up with the mended bridle and left.

That day we traveled up what seemed to be steeper hills than ever, and that night we camped under willow trees against the mountainside. This place was a little more sheltered than the other camps, and it was a good thing too, because it thundered and rained. I heard the rolling peals of thunder and saw the flashes of bright lightning even through the canvas of the tent.

While I did the supper dishes and pans at the little spring, I'd noticed that Mother was talking with Turlock. Now while the storm went on and we lay in our sleeping bags, she told me what they'd talked about. "Fayette, Mr. Turlock told me what I'd suspected that there are several homesteads tucked here and there in these hills. He said I could go to them and ask the people to be library outposts, but he thought I would be wasting time. He says he knows the people hereabouts."

I growled, because he seemed to be running our lives. "Maybe they know him too?"

"Undoubtedly they do if he knows them. He says they'd either refuse me or take the library books I leave and burn them for stove wood. The books would not be waiting when I came back for them. He says the people hereabouts have no use for books."

I said, "Burning library books would be against the law."

"Yes, it would. But I decided if Turlock wouldn't vouch for people he knew, it would not be wise of me to trust them with county property, would it?"

"No, I guess not. But where is Mr. Turlock willing to take you, Mother?"

"To Pickett's Crossing. He says it's not just one homestead but a place people come to. It's a third of the distance to Big Tree Junction and a good spot to rest for a time while I arrange for an outpost there."

Lying on the floor of the tent, listening to the rain fall on the top, I thought about the Possum. He appeared to be turning into the real boss of our mountain journey. I'd read *Heidi* several times and knew from experience that she hadn't ever met anybody like the Possum, a person with the look of a held-in volcano. I was stiff from riding a mule that didn't like me, dirty from not bathing for days or washing my clothing, and now we were going who knew where with him! And all that talk about porcupines and mule sweat! Who'd ever be hungry enough to eat a porcupine?

Though there was a thick mist the morning after the rain, it didn't stop Turlock from heading out through the hills. Even though he'd slept out of doors in his bedroll and had a dripping beard, the weather didn't seem to bother him. He was as spry as ever.

We had some oatmeal porridge and canned milk, hot

cocoa made from more canned milk, and graham crackers for breakfast before we mounted up. Then we sat on wet saddles on top of wet mules. I felt as if I were squishing with dampness as I rode along behind Mother. The trees that fringed the narrow trail were wet with rain. A person would think all the drops of water would be gone by the time the first seven mules and the horse had brushed past the branches, but that wasn't so. There was plenty to fall on me and Blackie as we rode by.

By late morning, the mist had disappeared and the sun came out hot on my back, so hot that steam rose from my mule's neck. We went over and down a big green hill, and then suddenly we were at a place where two trails came together. Beyond the trail lay five buildings, unpainted wooden ones, two much larger than the others. The big ones had a row of posts in front, porches, and signboards on their false fronts. One said *Pickett's Crossing General Store, Lydia Pickett, Proprietress and Postmistress;* the other said *The Only Chance Saloon, Sam Pickett, Prop.*

We had come to Pickett's Crossing, which was a saloon, a large store and post office, two sheds, and a little house with curtains at the window. I figured it was the home of Mr. and Mrs. Pickett.

We were the only people in sight. Not only weren't there any people around, there were no horses at the hitching rails. There wasn't any sound either. Then I saw a movement out of the side of my eye. It was Eubie. When I saw what he was up to, I tightened the reins of my mule fast.

"*Wah-h-h!*" came the sound of the trumpet blast.

95

As I figured, Blackie made a leap into the air, with all four hooves off the ground. Mother's mule also reared. So did the pack mules. The white mare turned about and went at a gallop between the saloon and general store, and an instant afterward Noah, Ham, Shem, and Japheth went charging after Hagar. Eubie's Ishmael followed his mother too, but first he bucked Eubie off onto the ground. Turlock didn't fall off, but he didn't stop to rescue my brother. He rode his mule after the others, leaving us Ashmores alone in Pickett's Crossing.

I got Blackie under control just as a man came running out of the saloon toward me, his arms flailing. Out of the general store came a tall, thin old lady with her apron fluttering. From where he sat on the ground, Eubie told them, "We're the Monterey library!"

"What the devil?" shouted the man, a big, portly, balding gink.

"What library did ya say?" asked the wizened-faced, gray-headed woman, who was glaring at Eubie.

Mother shouted, "Eubie, that was wrong!" Then, when she calmed her mule, she added, "I apologize for my son's behavior. I am Mrs. Lettie Ashmore. I'm a librarian from Monterey. I've brought you books from my library if you'd care to borrow them. They are on the pack animals that have just now run away, but I am quite sure they will soon be back among us."

The tall woman folded her arms. "We didn't order any books from anywhere. How come you're bringing them up here on mules?"

Mother explained about the library outposts she

wanted to set up and about the five Big Tree Junction ladies who were desperate for books.

When Mother had finished, the lady nodded, looking down at her shoes and up again. "You make some sense, I guess," she said. "All right, I'm Lydia Pickett. This is my husband, Sam. We're glad to meet ya. I guess I could be a library outpost for ya in my store and post office, unless Sam wants to have the books in his saloon. Books could attract customers to us both, I reckon."

Clearly not wanting to tell Mr. Wallace that she had set up a library outpost in a saloon, Mother said slowly, "Well, I don't know. Tell me, which of the two places do most people from this part of the mountains visit?"

"It's half and half," explained Mr. Pickett. "Lydia gets all of the womenfolks and kids. I get the menfolks. The women don't come to my place, and some of the men don't ever set foot in Lydia's. They let the women get all they need in the way of supplies."

His answer gave me an idea. "Why don't you split up the books?" I asked Mother. "Give the kind that ladies and kids like to the store and the men's kind to the saloon."

"That's good," said Eubie, who was on his feet now.

"Well, I suppose I could do it that way," agreed Mother, who was smiling because the Picketts were so agreeable.

Everyone was smiling by the time Mr. Turlock reappeared from behind the shed. He was leading Hagar, and the pack mules were trailing along behind her. Eubie's mule walked beside the horse.

I saw the Picketts turn to stare at the parade, and I watched Turlock ride slowly up to them and halt.

Nobody said a word until Mr. Pickett said, "Howdy, Gil. Lydia and me heard you'd come back to the mountains."

"Yep, I'm back."

"How long ya been back?" asked Mrs. Pickett, with a quick glance at us Ashmores.

"Some time now, but not in this part of the country."

There was a silence that Mother interrupted. "I hired Mr. Turlock as my library mule driver on the way here after Mr. Denver Murfree, my first driver, had an accident."

Mr. Pickett asked, "What kind of accident did Denver have?"

"He cut his foot with an ax. He's being taken care of at the Mackenzie homestead."

Mrs. Pickett now spoke to us Ashmores. "Well, that's too bad. All right, you library folks get down and come into the store with me and have a chat."

"Thank you, we will," said Mother. Then she asked Turlock, "Will you see to the animals?"

"That's what I'm here for!"

As I dismounted, I wondered if Mr. Pickett was going to invite Turlock into his saloon for something, but he didn't. He gave Turlock a grim look, took a plug of tobacco out of his shirt pocket, bit into it, and turned on his heel, going back into his saloon. No, he didn't want any part of the Possum, and neither did his wife. They knew him from other times. What did they know? Whatever it was, I intended to find out.

I also intended to leave the Edgar Allan Poe book behind in Pickett's Crossing. It didn't matter one bit to me whether it stayed at the general store or the saloon, so long as it stayed while we went on. There being two outpost places here doubled my chances of getting rid of "The Fall of the House of Usher."

Mrs. Pickett's store was full of things—not only canned goods, but thread, bolts of cloth, yarn, barrels of pickles and crackers, farm tools, a coffee-grinding machine, horse gear, pots and pans, picks and shovels, patent medicines, and three big glass jars of hard candy on a counter.

Eubie and I didn't stay inside with Mother and Mrs. Pickett, because the minute Mrs. Pickett gave each of us a peppermint stick she shooed us out to sit on the porch. "Before my husband and I pick out the books we think would do best around here, I want to talk private with your mama. Little pitchers have big ears."

How I hated that old saying grown-ups used so much! But to keep the peace I went out and sat down on the top step with Eubie. I could plot how to get rid of the hoodoo book better outside where it was quiet. Eubie didn't stay with me. He wandered off to where Mr. Turlock and the animals stood at the side of the Pickett woodshed.

I sucked on my peppermint stick and thought hard. By the time Mother and Mrs. Pickett were through talking, I'd figured a possible way to make sure that Mr. Edgar Allan Poe was left behind in Pickett's Crossing.

The Picketts hopped right to the job of selecting the books they wanted after Mother, Eubie, and I had unpacked the saddlebags. Turlock didn't have any part in the library work. He'd taken the mules and Hagar over to the watering trough beside the barn and was currying them with a brush and inspecting their hooves for stones.

As the Picketts pawed over the books, I glanced now and then at the Possum, who was acting as if nothing mattered but the animals. Finally Mrs. Pickett put her stack of books in one of the two wheelbarrows Mr. Pickett had brought out of her store, and he put his in the other.

I went over to look at both stacks in the wheelbarrows. Mrs. Pickett disappointed me. She didn't have the Poe book on her pile. For a moment, I had high hopes that Mr. Pickett, bless him, had taken the book, because he had a skinny black one on top of his choices. But when I looked closer and read its spine, I saw that it was *Great Crimes of Old London*.

Looking around, I saw that the Poe book was nearby, on top of a pile Mother was about to repack. I'd have to move fast to make my plan work. I went over to her stack, got the book, and, with my eyes squinted up, brought "The Fall of the House of Usher" over to Mrs. Pickett. Handing it to her, I said, "This is full of real good stories. I bet you or one of the other mountain ladies would like it."

"Mebbe so. Mebbe I would."

To my joy, she took it and opened it, running her finger down the list of stories. Then she made my heart sink by closing it with a snap and handing it back to me.

"No, girlie, I don't want this here book," she told me. "The print's too little for my eyes. What's more, I see it's got a story called 'The Gold Bug' in it. I don't want my husband to see that. He's inclined to gold fever as it is. It's because of gold we come up here twenty years back. Sam still thinks there's gold hereabouts and won't leave because of it. No, girlie, I like books with mushy love stories in them."

I saw her look over my head; then she poked me in the bosom just as Turlock walked past us with a saddlebag. I said, "Huh?" as I stepped backward from her.

She spoke to me in a voice so low she was whispering, and I had to come up close to hear her. "Open your eyes and stop that squinty bus'ness. I tried to warn your mama that the mule skinner you got with ya ain't the sort of person a library lady and her kids ought to keep comp'ny with. Your mama says she knows about him and she ain't worried. She wouldn't pay any heed to me, so I'm telling you."

Here was my chance. I glanced at Mother, who was busy making a list of the books each of the Picketts took, just as she had at the Mackenzie homestead. She had her back to us and was out of earshot. I whispered back, "What's wrong with Mr. Turlock?"

"Plenty!" Mrs. Pickett's eyes rolled behind her spectacles as she looked at the sky. Then she spoke to me again, this time in a hiss. "Plenty, but it's not for me to tell ya. The best thing for you folks to do if Turlock gives ya trouble is to use the telegraph line wherever ya find it in the hills and wire the Monterey sheriff. You should get hold of him if Turlock does it again."

"Does what, Mrs. Pickett?"

"Does what he did before! I don't want to say any more, because I don't want to upset a poor little tyke like you. Anyway, I got to go now."

Old as she was, she could move fast. She went to her wheelbarrow of books, grabbed hold of its handles, and started to trundle it to her store. Mother ran after her and, catching up, explained how she should keep records for the library when she loaned books out.

I looked from Mother to Mr. Pickett, who was following his wife, and then from him to Turlock, who was tending to the pack mules. He'd soon be bringing the freshly curried mules over and loading their saddlebags on them again.

Eubie was repacking books. I went over to him and put the Poe book into one of the big leather bags that had been set on the ground for the Picketts to look through, because Mrs. Pickett had said she had bad rheumatism in her arms and couldn't reach high.

Should I tell Eubie what I'd heard here? No, I'd better not. I'd keep it to myself until tonight when I was in the tent with Mother. Then I'd ask her what she knew about the Possum that I didn't know. What was he? A suspected robber, an outlaw? Or maybe a crazy man? He sure didn't seem normal to me.

I dropped to my knees and started to help Eubie stuff books into the nearest saddlebag as he complained to me, "Fayette, aren't we going to be invited to stay for supper and overnight here too?"

"No, it doesn't look like it, does it."

"No, but I sort of figured Mr. Pickett would ask me and Turlock inside his saloon."

"Ask you, Eubie?" I laughed. "You're only eleven years old, Herbert Percival Ashmore."

He flared up. "I could drink sarsparilla or ginger ale in there."

I said, "It appears to me that Mr. Pickett doesn't want the company of either one of you."

"But I never been inside a saloon!" Eubie mourned.

I comforted him. "Oh, Eubie, you've seen lots of cowboy movies, so you ought to know what saloons look like inside. They're all the same in all the movies we go to."

"Well," Eubie said with a sniff, "I guess it doesn't matter to the Possum. He isn't like Mr. Murfree. He doesn't drink. When I told him the other day that Malindy left us one bottle of whiskey for the mare, he said Hagar was welcome to it. He doesn't touch a drop anymore."

That, at least, was one good thing to hear about Turlock. As I went on packing, I heard a clop-clop sound behind me of a pack mule he was bringing to us. We'd soon be on our way out of Pickett's Crossing. And what next? What had I got us into with all my fibbing and scheming down in Monterey? Right now the Hillman

103

sisters and Mr. Herbert appeared easier to deal with back home than the Possum on the trail.

After he'd got the book bags onto the mules again, we mounted up. Just before we started off, I heard the Possum say to Mother, "You'd better tell your boy not to blow that bugle of his anymore. The mules don't like it."

Mother said, "You are quite right. Eubie, you leave the bugle alone from now on."

Eubie answered, "Okay, I won't touch Dad's old bugle, but it isn't because I don't want to."

Mother said, "Eubie, there are far too many bugles being blown in war overseas. I think we can do without that sound up here in the peace of the mountains."

Peace? I looked at her. How could she have thought Pickett's Crossing was peaceful with the mules running away? She clicked her tongue at Brownie and gave him his head, and Blackie and I dropped behind her as usual. She was sure acting strangely. No, I didn't think it was going to be easy to pry information about the Possum out of her. Like a lot of mothers, she had a stubborn streak in her nature. Well, I'd try her again after we camped for the night, when she and I were alone.

Turlock took the trail that wound south, or at least I thought it was south, out of Pickett's Crossing. It led us down the side of a mountain until late afternoon, when he stopped in a little green valley with big forested hills on each side of it.

He'd brought us to a place with people again. I saw a good-size house set in the middle of the valley beside a brook that ran through the wild oats and grass like a silver ribbon. Turlock rode back to speak to Mother. "This here's a new homestead, and I don't know the folks," he said, "but old man Mackenzie told me about 'em. He says the man and woman here keep a bunch of orphan kids to help 'em out. Mackenzie says he figgered that they might be wantin' books for the young'uns they got."

Mother said, "Well, I suppose I could sound them out about being an outpost. All they can do is say No."

The Possum said, "They could shoot ya, but I doubt they will." He drew out the rifle from its saddle holster, raised it, and fired it three times. To my surprise, the mules didn't budge. They were bugle shy, but not gun shy. Turlock waited till the echo of the shots was over, then said, "That's a signal mountain people use when they're comin' in or when there's trouble."

Mother said, "That's good to know."

We wound down through the tall pasture grass to the house, where a group of people stood on the porch, waiting for us. There was a big, yellow-bearded man with a rifle cradled in his arms; a tall, heavy-set, black-haired lady; and six kids in overalls, all boys and all different looking. The orphans, for sure!

The man demanded, "Who'd you folks be?"

Mother took charge, telling her business for the library, and giving him all our names.

"Books? You brung us books?" exclaimed the woman. She laughed, then elbowed the man in the ribs. "Gideon, they've got books on them mules, books from down in Monterey!" She laughed again and added, "They want to make a liberry out of ya and me and this passel of brats we got. Well, you best not stop here, lady, 'cause Gideon and me can't do more than sign our names. Books is worthless to us."

Suddenly the biggest boy, who must have been my age, said, "I can read! So can two of the others." He sounded proud. "We learned how to read in the orphan home before Mr. and Mrs. Phipenny fetched us up here with 'em. My name's Joshua, Joshua Drucker. I used to favor reading when I had something to read."

"So did I," said the boy next to Joshua.

I watched Mother hesitate, then as I squinted I saw her ride closer to the porch up to Mrs. Phipenny. "Well, then, could Joshua Drucker and this other boy take care of the books for the library so your neighbors could borrow them?" she asked, leaning down. "It isn't difficult. I could show the boys how, and on my way back here to Monterey I'd pick up the books and have others sent here by mail."

Gideon Phipenny boomed, "We don't get no mail! We haven't got any neighbors that come here. No, my wife and me don't want to get mixed up in no more county or state bus'ness. Homesteadin' this place is enough to work for her and me. We haven't got time for book folderol."

"Books are not folderol," said Mother firmly, sitting on her mule as if it had been a beautiful, thoroughbred steed.

"Aw right, then," interrupted Turlock, "how about lettin' our animals graze here and us camp here overnight?"

Mr. and Mrs. Phipenny spoke to one another, and then he said, "Camp over yonder beside the corral. Yer animals are welcome to the grass but not to any of our hay or oats, and it'll cost you two dollars to use the creek water." Oh, but the Phipennys were money grabbers.

I hoped Mother would tell the man No and we'd go on, but she didn't. She asked Turlock, "What do you think?"

"Pay him. We might as well stay here rather'n make camp after dark. It appears old man Mackenzie made a mistake, don't it?"

"Yes, it does." Mother spoke next to the Phipennys. "I'll give you the money as soon as we've dismounted."

Phipenny gave Joshua Drucker a shove toward us. "There's no need to come back here with the money. We're eatin' supper, and it's gettin' cold on the table. I hate grub that's got cold. Give Joshua the money, and he'll show ya where to pitch yer tents."

Joshua jumped down off the porch and went at a run toward the corral beside the unpainted new barn. My, but he was skinny! He was polite, too. He helped Mother and me down off our mules and stood waiting, even after she had given him two dollars.

While Turlock started to make camp, unsaddling and unpacking the mules and mare, Eubie came up to him. "How long have you been here?" he asked Joshua.

"Three years now. I was the first orphan they got hold of. I helped while they were buildin' the house and barn."

"Where did you come from before that?" I asked him.

"Hollister. That's where I lived till my pa died and I

went to the orphan home. My ma died when I was born."

Joshua had long, dark-red hair and a bony face, white-skinned and freckled like Eubie's. It was a nice face, smart-looking, I thought.

Mother said, "It's very pretty up here. Do you like it?"

He gave her a sad look, shook his head, and started slowly for the house with the two dollars.

Mother sighed and turned to Eubie and me. "Be glad you aren't orphans."

"Well, we are half orphans, you know," Eubie reminded her.

"I know. I know. It's never out of my mind for a moment that your father is gone." Mother looked thoughtful, and I knew that she was thinking of Mr. Herbert. Probably he looked good to her right now. She made a shooing motion with her hands. "Go see if you can't do something to aid Mr. Turlock if he'll permit it, Eubie, while Fayette and I pick out the canned goods for our supper and breakfast. I see that Turlock's got the pack off Hagar."

While Mother and I went through the cans, picking out peaches and beans, I found my chance to talk with her. "Mother, Mrs. Pickett warned me about the Possum. She said to get word to the sheriff in Monterey about him if he makes trouble. She told me he was bad."

She wasn't looking at me but at a can that had lost its label. "I wonder what this one is. More peaches or more beans? Yes, Fayette, Mrs. Pickett had some notions regarding Mr. Turlock."

"But, Mother, she and her husband *know* him! We don't!"

"I grant you that they may have known him longer, but even so their opinions of him are not necessarily gospel truth. I am not inclined to accept what Mrs. Pickett thinks about him or what they think I should do. I agree with you that his personal appearance is against him, but under all that hair he must have a human face."

I told her, "Maybe not."

"Don't be silly, Fayette. He is a man who has had an unfortunate history, one Mr. Mackenzie told me. Mackenzie thought Turlock was the man to get the books through the mountains."

"But Mr. Mackenzie was wrong about the Phipennys."

"Yes." She was shaking the can now to see if she had solid beans or loose peaches. "But he was right about children being here." She put the can down. "It shakes like peaches. I wish we could do something about these poor waifs here. I believe the Phipennys have them only to work the way Mr. Turlock was worked as a boy. Surely the Phipennys are not sending these boys to school. The youngest ones will very likely never learn to read."

I moved closer to her. "Report them to the school people down in Monterey when we get home, so they have to get the boys taught and see that they have books."

"I have already thought of that, Fayette. As a lawyer, Mr. Herbert will be able to tell me how to go about it."

Him again? Well, maybe I could do something for the boys too. And then an idea came to me. I could leave a book as a gift, and Joshua could read it to them.

Glory be, I had just the book in mind—a thin, black one in Shem's saddlebag at this very moment. Oh, this was good, very good. We wouldn't be coming back here, so I wouldn't ever have to set eyes on that Edgar Allan Poe book again.

Though I hadn't got anywhere asking Mother about the Possum and had plenty to worry about, I slept just fine that night. Even the coyotes howling in the hills and the Phipennys' dog barking to keep the coyotes company didn't disturb me. Every time a coyote or a dog yelp woke me up, I went right back to sleep.

When morning came, Mother cooked breakfast and I cleaned up after it as usual. Then I went over to Shem's saddlebag, reached in, and got out the Poe book. I watched until I saw Mr. Phipenny, the dog, and all the boys trail into the barn. Mrs. Phipenny had finished sweeping the front porch and gone inside. Then I ran up to the porch, put the Poe book on the ground under it, and ran back to our camp. Somebody would look under the porch before long, but not before we'd left.

As we rode out of Phipenny Valley, our mules wading through the shallow brook, I turned around midstream to look back at the house. Mrs. Phipenny stood on the porch, leaning on her broom, watching us go. She wasn't waving any book in the air to attract our notice. Glory be, I had got rid of "The Fall of the House of Usher," the curse of the Ashmores! Joshua Drucker might even

110

enjoy owning it and remember us kindly for leaving it behind. After all, it did have some very fine tales in it besides the one Miss Uffelman had read. I hoped I hadn't hoodooed Joshua by leaving Mr. Poe with him, but the time had come for that book to find a real home, not a library. I hoped it would bring Joshua some good luck and show him that somebody thought well enough of him to leave a present. I was sure he didn't get many from the Phipennys. This morning two of the other orphan boys had had black eyes that they hadn't had the night before.

My spirits brightened. Maybe now that we'd got rid of our hoodoo our luck would change. Maybe we'd get rid of Mr. Turlock and find a nice, civilized mule driver to replace him. Even if Mother wouldn't tell me what she knew about him, I was pretty sure she wouldn't mind changing to somebody else who knew mules.

That day we climbed another mountain and at sunset camped at a place that was very interesting, even if there weren't any people there. It was a hot springs, a spot where water came up out of the ground in steaming pools. We could smell it on the breeze, a sort of bad egg odor, before we even saw it.

As Turlock led the mule train up to the pools, Mother exclaimed in joy, "A bath! We can all have a hot bath at last. Mr. Turlock, are the pools safe to bathe in?"

"Yep," he called back to her, "but don't drink the water. I'll have to take the mules to a pond a half mile from here. Yer boy can come with me and get water for yer cookin' and fetch it back."

"Eubie, go with him," Mother said. Then she turned around and called to me, "Fayette, get off Blackie. You and I will bathe while Mr. Turlock and Eubie take the animals on ahead."

I stayed on Blackie, looking at the Possum. Then I rode up to Eubie and said quietly, "Turlock told you not to blow Dad's bugle, but if you see him start heading back here before you think we've had time to bathe, please blow it to warn us to get out of the water."

Eubie looked doubtful, then said, "Okay, but I don't think he'd do that."

"You don't know what he'd do. There's an awful lot about him we don't know."

"All right, I'll blow the trumpet if I have to. Just don't hang around in the water too long."

"Are you scared of the wild gink too, Eubie?"

"Not as much as I was, but I can't say I'm real easy with him yet."

"That's using your head."

I rode back to Mother. "It probably won't take long to water the animals," I told her. "I think we'd better not figure on a long soak."

She smiled at me, dismounted, and gave the reins of her mule to Eubie. He waited for me to get off Blackie and then rode away, hauling both mules behind him.

Mother held up her hand. There was a cake of soap in it. She said, "There won't be any towels, Fayette, or any clean clothing, but at least we'll be clean underneath."

I looked past her at the pools where the steam rose in long, gray streamers. We'd be clean underneath all

112

right, but just how hot was this water and what would we smell like afterward? I didn't want to wash my hair in water that smelled like bad eggs.

I didn't undress and jump right into the nearest pool. First I went to each one and stuck a finger in to see which had the best temperature for a bath. Then I broke off a thin branch from a tree, stripped off the leaves, and stuck it into the coolest pool to see how deep it was. After all, a person could drown in the mountains as well as at the beach! Finally I got out of my duds and, holding onto a tree root that went into the pool, slid down into the water, finding a place to sit down.

Mother slid in beside me, soaped herself, closed her eyes, and said, "Oh, this is glorious! I can feel every muscle and sinew unwinding. I've been so stiff."

Glorious? I wasn't so sure of that. As I used the soap too, my ears were straining to hear the bugle and my nose was not one bit happy with the smell of the mineral bath.

Mother murmured, "I bet the Indians have bathed here for centuries."

I told her, "If they ate eggs, they could have boiled 'em in the pool over there."

She didn't hear me. I'd returned the soap to her, and she was ducking her head under the water. She came up with it wet and shampooed her hair; then she gave me the soap and said, "Wash your hair, Fayette."

I did, though I didn't want to. I hoped the lavender scent of the soap would help cover up the smell of the water, but I doubted it.

Mother said before she submerged herself again, "How delightful! How relaxing it is here in the wilderness! Don't you enjoy this, Fayette?"

"Uh-huh," I told her, listening for Eubie's bugle. He never did blow it, and we were out and dried and dressed before he and the Possum came back.

Because Mother insisted, Eubie had a bath later on too. Whether Mr. Turlock bathed after we went into our tents, I never did know. The way he looked, he could have any number of baths and who would know the difference?

The sound of birds, an awful lot of them, woke me at dawn. I glanced over at Mother, who was deep asleep in her sleeping bag, rolled away to the side of the tent, and lifted up the bottom edge to look out. What I saw made me suck in my breath in astonishment.

The Terrible Turlock was sitting on the fallen log we had used as a seat during supper last night. His big hands were on his knees, and his head was tilted back, looking up into the sky, whistling. He was making some of the bird noises. Most of the other sounds were real. The log was covered with dozens of little hopping brown birds, and the ground around his feet was full of them too. He wasn't throwing food to them, only whistling to them, and they were answering him. He seemed to be almost talking to them. I waited to see if one would land on him, but none did. Yet they were all about him.

And then I heard Eubie cough from the tent on the other side of ours. That one sound made all the birds flutter up into the air. In an instant they were all gone. The next moment the Possum got up too and walked over to renew the fire he'd banked last night to keep it smoldering till morning.

I let go of the tent's canvas and rolled back toward the center. Mother was sitting up, looking at me. "What did you see out there, Fayette?" she asked.

"The Possum and a whole flock of little birds. He was whistling to them."

Mother laughed and said, "Yes, Mr. Mackenzie said he has quite a way with animals and birds."

I grumbled, "You were told a lot of things Eubie and I weren't."

"That's right."

"You used to tell me everything. You told me about you and Mr. Herbert. What did Mr. Mackenzie tell you about Turlock?"

Her voice was firm as she got out of her sleeping bag. "That is my business, Fayette—mine, Turlock's, and Mr. Mackenzie's."

"Does Turlock know that you know things about him?" I asked.

"I should think so. He'd expect Mr. Mackenzie to speak to me of him, and I spoke to him myself at the Mackenzie house." She had started to unbraid her hair so she could comb and coil it for the day. "Fayette, please don't pester me with questions about him and don't upset Eubie about him either."

"All right, I won't." I was mad. I didn't tell her that I was keeping my eyes peeled for a telegraph pole and by now was wondering if Turlock wasn't taking us by trails the telegraph lines didn't come to. Maybe the big galoot could whistle birds out of the sky and not hurt them, but he still wasn't any saint. In my personal opinion, his bird whistling was just plain spine-chilling.

After climbing up from the hot springs, we followed the ridge of a mountain for miles in the hot sun for most of the day. In all that time, we didn't see another human being. Oh, but this was lonesome country, even if it was pretty. At times, it could be dangerous, too, because the mountainside would fall steeply away from the trail. Tiny rocks dislodged by our passing mules were kicked over the edge and went rattling down and down hundreds of feet below. When we came to those places, I'd close my eyes, pray, and let my mule pick his way over the trail, all the while hating to trust myself to a mule's mind as Turlock had told us to do. "Mules are surefooted by nature," he said. "Give yer critter his head, and he'll take ya over. Don't mess with him on a tight place with a drop to it. Trust yer mule."

There were four scarey places on the ridge, but we passed them all safely and then went down into another valley, surrounded on all sides by hills. There were buildings here too, another homestead with a barn and woodshed. I'd already figured there'd be people nearby, because I'd heard rifle shots in the distance. Somebody was probably out hunting. There had been nine shots in all, three at a time, and then another nine of them in groups of threes.

Once more Turlock fired Murfree's rifle three times

up into the air. He was answered at once by three shots from the farmhouse.

Turlock frowned and cried out to us, "Stay where you are. There's somethin' wrong here. Somebody's comin'."

Trouble? What kind of trouble? It surely looked peaceful.

But somebody was coming toward us, walking very fast and carrying a rifle. He was a middle-aged man with a lined face and dark hair streaked with gray. As I squinted to welcome him, I saw him come up to Turlock and noticed that like Mr. Pickett he didn't offer to shake hands. Did he know Turlock by reputation too? He didn't seem unfriendly, though he didn't smile.

The two men spoke quietly together while the mules switched their tails and Eubie's lowered its head to crop the high green grass of the meadow. Finally the homesteader left, walking back to the house, looking down at the grass as he went. My squinting had been for nothing. He hadn't taken any more note of me or my squint than the Phipennys had. I let my eyes open wide again.

Turlock rode up to us now and said, "There's trouble here aw right. It's sickness."

Mother asked, "Do you know the people?"

"Nope, I don't know the man, but his wife was kin to my ma's folks. I knew her when she was a little girl."

Mother asked, "What kind of sickness is it? Did the homesteader tell you? Is it cholera?"

"Nope, he says it's not that one. He knows about it. He thinks it come from a traveler who brought it with him and died of it here. He said it's a high fever."

117

"Probably typhoid fever," said Mother. "Do they have a stream or a well?"

"A well. I asked him. He says they quit usin' it since his youngest gal died right after his wife did."

"Good Lord, both of them!" Mother exclaimed. "Are there others sick?"

"His boy, the oldest one, passed away this mornin'. Him and the other boy are aw right so far. He's been shootin' his rifle all day, hopin' somebody would hear and fetch someone who knows how to heal sickness. He hoped you'd be a travelin' nurse or the circuit-ridin' doctor."

I saw Mother, who had been slumped in her saddle straighten up. "I wish we were, Mr. Turlock. Still, there are medical books in the saddlebags. Perhaps we can help these poor people with them?"

"Mebbe the books can, missus, but you can't go inside that house."

"Can't I, Mr. Turlock?"

"No, the fever's mighty catchin'. The man won't let ya in. He said if ya wasn't a trained nurse for ya to ride away from here and get a nurse to come."

"But I could leave a medical book for him. Can he read?"

"I don't know. I didn't ask him."

"Well, I will." I saw Mother nudge her mule into a trot that took it over the meadow toward the house.

Turlock turned to Eubie and me. "You two stay right here", he ordered. "I'm goin' after yer ma."

I didn't even think of disobeying him and was glad that he planned to go after Mother. Another thought made me freeze. Would the homesteader shoot her if she tried to get into the house? But she stayed outside. From where we were I could hear her shouting at the man, but I couldn't hear what he said in reply. Mr. Turlock, who sat on his mule beside her, didn't shout at all and didn't move a muscle that I could see. A lot of help he was!

Then Mother came riding back and dismounted. She called to me, "The homesteader can read. He says he'll take a medical book and a copy of the Bible. Come, help me find them."

"Yes." I got off Blackie and searched with her through the saddlebags until we found what she wanted.

By the time we were through, Turlock had returned too and dismounted. He went to the white mare and, while we held the books, got the shovel off her load. Then he told us, "There was more said after ya left, ma'am. I been asked to dig the grave for the oldest boy, and the man would like ya to say some words over him and the others he buried himself. He'd do the diggin', but he ain't had any sleep for three days while he's been tendin' to the boy who died, and he don't know if he's got the strength for it."

Mother gave me, then Eubie, a very sad look, nodded, and said, "Of course, I'll say a burial service here. There are prayer books in the saddlebags too, and I'll read the twenty-third psalm."

She gave us a mournful little smile. "There's something for every occasion and person in the library's selection of books, it seems. But then Mr. Wallace, who picked out most of the books, knows these mountains, so he figured what would be needed." She nodded grimly. "Well, libraries are to serve the people! Fayette, you look for the prayer books. I think there should be several of them scattered about in the bags, small red books. Get three out if you can find them, so we Ashmores can each have one." She asked Turlock, "What is the name of the family here?"

"Rogers, what's left of 'em." Turlock went with the shovel over his shoulder, and Mother walked behind him carrying the big, dark-green medical book and the black Bible. I watched her go to the house, set the books down on the porch, and disappear around the side of it with Turlock. Then I set about finding three copies of the same prayer book in the saddlebags, which proved to be easy. Putting them aside, I sat down in the meadow with Eubie, who held the halter rope of the white mare, as she and the mules grazed. The meadow was beautiful, full of tall purple, white, and yellow flowers. After a time, I got up and picked an armful of them.

Mother came back alone. "Children, come on now. Mr. Turlock is at the grave he dug. Mr. Rogers was bringing his boy out as I left. He says he'll be ready for us in a few minutes." She saw my armful of flowers and nodded at me. Her cheeks were wet, but she wiped them with her jacket sleeve and bent to pick up a copy of the prayer book. She opened it to the index, saying, "The burial service is on page forty-four. I'll read it aloud, and you read the responses along with me as if you're a church congregation."

"What'll we do with the mules?" Eubie asked.

"Leave them with Hagar. They won't stray from

where the grazing is so good. Now listen to me, children. Do not go near the house or Mr. Rogers or the little boy. They'll be on one side of the oldest boy's grave during the services, and we'll be on the other. Mr. Turlock will fill in the grave. Then we'll leave here at once."

I asked, "And we'll look for a doctor or nurse to come as soon as we can?"

"Yes, of course, as soon as we can. And we pray it won't be too late for Mr. Rogers and the small boy. Rogers is not using the water from the well, which we think the stranger polluted with typhoid when he used the family dipper. He is going up into the hills to a spring he knows. Now let's go."

Leaving the mules, we walked together over the meadow and around the house, which had a stack of white deer antlers as a front yard decoration, to the tiny graveyard a distance behind the woodshed. Three new graves, heaped with earth, were there, and one empty hole in the ground. Turlock stood on one side of it, where the dirt was piled high. On the other side stood Mr. Rogers and a small, yellow-haired, weeping boy, younger than Eubie.

Mother came to stand next to Turlock, and Eubie and I ranged ourselves on her left.

Mr. Rogers said, "I'd be pleased, ma'am, if you'd sing a bit too, for Tad and the others."

"Of course, I will."

Mother, who had once been a choir singer when she was a girl, had a nice voice. She sang "Abide with Me." Then she read the burial service from the prayer book, with Eubie and me giving the responses, including all the names as Mr. Rogers told them to her. Afterward she started to sing "Leaning on the Everlasting Arm."

When Mr. Rogers began singing that old hymn with her, so did Eubie and I because we knew the words too. Mr. Turlock, I noticed, didn't sing at all.

Then Mother read the twenty-third psalm from the Bible, as Eubie and I recited it by heart. At the end, she knelt down and picked up some of the dirt, letting it fall out of her hand onto the grave of the boy who lay down there covered in a gray blanket. The services were over.

Mr. Rogers said, "Thank you kindly, ma'am," and steering his boy by the shoulders, went into the house through the back door.

We Ashmores waited while Turlock shoveled dirt into the grave, filling it. Then I went up to it and laid some of my flowers on the top. The rest I put on the other graves. Finally the four of us walked away, passing the house, over the meadow and up to the mules and horse, every one of them a blur to me through my tears.

Eubie and I hadn't gone to our father's funeral in Monterey, because Mother had thought we were too young and had wanted to spare us. But we'd been to a funeral now, a funeral of a stranger we'd never even seen. We'd even taken part in it. Half of me felt very sad and worried over the two Rogers who were left. The other half felt proud that we had helped where we could and proud that the library had helped too. I just wished we could have done more.

As I mounted again and looked up at the mountains, I told myself that I wouldn't ever be the same again. Neither would Eubie.

6

The first thing Mother called out to us as she got onto her mule was, "We've got to find a telegraph line now. When we do, we'll climb up to it and send a message to Monterey. There could be a book in the saddlebags that will tell us how to send a message from a pole. Fayette, maybe you can climb up to the wire?"

Me, climb a pole or a tree? I didn't like high places. By rights, the Possum, who was a noted tree sitter, ought to volunteer for the job. He didn't, though. Oh, what had I got us all into? I vowed I wouldn't meddle in anybody's affairs ever again. Even trying to do good could backfire on meddlers.

When we camped that night, Mother looked through the library saddlebags until she found a book that had the Morse Code in it and some instructions on how to send a message by telegraph key. It was a book the Boy Scouts had published, and it was just full of stuff about camping out and living in the wilds. But there wasn't anything in that book about getting up to the telegraph wires to send messages without a clicker key.

After supper Mother asked the Possum, "What shall we do to help the Rogers family if we can't find a telegraph office?"

He muttered over his coffee cup, "The best thing is to tell the first person we meet on the trail to tell whoever he meets to pass the word along to a telegraph office somewhere to send a message to a doctor to come to the Rogers homestead. I don't know where telegraph offices are these days, because I ain't been in these parts for so long."

Mother sighed and said, "Mr. Turlock, that's a terrible communications system indeed."

"Ma'am, it's all I can think of right off." He sipped his coffee again. "This ain't like Monterey. These hills are out of the world. Things are diff'runt here. I bet ya never talk about feudin', do ya, though ya talk about that war a long ways off? There's a diff'runce for ya right there."

I caught at the word *feud*. I'd read about feuds in books like *Lorna Doone* and *Romeo and Juliet* and in the stories about the Ozark mountain families and the Scottish clans. Had Turlock turned into a hermit because of a feud up here? I wanted to ask but didn't.

Eubie, however, asked him point-blank, "Have you got anything to do with feuds? Are you part of a feuding family?"

"I dunno, boy. Mebbe I am. That's one of the reasons I'm willin' to go to Big Tree Junction with ya—to find out."

I caught my breath. What was he getting us Ashmores into now? Would we be caught up in a blood feud with him?

Eubie went on asking questions. "What's the name of the family you might be feuding with?"

"Gordon."

"Where are they?" Eubie wanted to know.

"All over the hills. There are lots of 'em."

Eubie asked, "What started the feud?"

"Me, I did."

Mother said very sharply now, "Eubie! That is enough. Don't pry so much into Mr. Turlock's business. You're making a nuisance of yourself. Go brush your teeth and get ready for bed, while Fayette washes the dishes and pots and pans at the spring."

Yes, we were being got rid of when the conversation was getting interesting and I was learning something. Slowly Eubie and I left the campfire as Mother went back to talking about Mr. Rogers and his little boy and our chances of finding somebody along the trail tomorrow to help them.

Oh, that night was a wicked one. I couldn't fall asleep, because my mind was on the Rogers family and their terrible troubles. And when I finally did, the ground under me began shaking so terribly that I woke up right away again. "Mother, what is it?" I cried out.

Her voice came out of the dark, "It's an earthquake, Fayette."

I asked her, terrified, "What'll we do *up here*?" I knew about quakes. In Monterey, when we had one, we ran to get under a desk or table or went to stand in a doorway, the strongest part of a building. But what did people do out of doors in a tent?

"Nothing. Go back to sleep. There's nothing to hurt us here, not even if the tent falls on us."

Then another quaking started under me, a rolling tremor that made me slide in my sleeping bag closer to the center of the tent, grab the pole, and hold onto it, so it couldn't fall down.

Suddenly I heard a sort of muffled yelping from nearby and Eubie's voice crying, "Help! Get me out from under here!"

I shouted to Mother, "It's Eubie. His tent must have fallen down on him. What'll we do? He might smother."

"Fayette, stick your head out and call to Eubie. Tell him to wriggle out from under his tent and come over here."

While the earth rocked under me, I braced myself on my hands and knees, called to Eubie, and watched by moonlight as he squirmed under the canvas of his tent and finally slithered out, dragging his sleeping bag. He crawled over to our tent, pushed past me as another, smaller shock struck, and came inside.

"Now both of you go to sleep," Mother ordered calmly. "Nobody is hurt."

I asked, "Where's the Possum?"

"Out in the woods, like always," Eubie announced.

Mother said, "Settle down and try to sleep."

After I got into my sleeping bag again, I found that I couldn't sleep. I listened to Mother's soft breathing, then heard Eubie's rustling, reedy breath, but I didn't fall off myself. I kept my hand on the tent pole so our tent couldn't go down too, waiting for more tremors that never did come.

• • •

Mother asked me as we mounted up the next morning, "Did you pray for the Rogers family last night, Fayette?"

"Yes, and I prayed for us too, the way I always do, and for that boy Joshua who isn't happy, and for the Mackenzies."

She told me, "I prayed that we'd meet somebody on the trail today who can send aid to the Rogers."

"I hope we do, and I sure hope they aren't named Gordon," I couldn't resist adding.

She gave me a strange glance as she mounted her mule. I'd noticed that she didn't hunt for a fallen tree or a stump to stand on anymore before she got onto Brownie. For a lady her age, she was getting more and more limber. She didn't act as if she ached so much from riding all day long either. That hot springs bath probably helped, but I supposed the exercise and fresh air were the main reasons she felt so well. I felt the same way myself, good in health though worried in mind.

That day we rode along high ridges, so we let the mules have their heads again. I couldn't honestly say that I liked Blackie, who had a bad habit of turning his head around to look at me and stretching his lips toward my boot. Still, even if he clicked his teeth as if to get a bite of my toes, I trusted him in high places. I figured that he didn't want to fall down ravines any more than I did.

Though I kept a constant watch for telegraph wires, I didn't spy any where we went, and I was getting more and more puzzled. By now I suspected the Possum plenty! No, sir, I didn't trust him any farther than I could throw him, which wasn't far since I couldn't even lift him.

In midafternoon we descended into a gloomy gulch strewn with big, moss-covered rocks among the tall evergreen trees. A little stream was running over and around more rocks at the bottom. It was cool down there among the trees after the heat of the high ridges, a good place to take a rest, stretch our legs, and water the animals.

I'd just got off Blackie and was watching him drinking beside me at the brook while I ate a crumbling soda cracker from my shirt pocket when it happened. A bullet hit the boulder behind me—*ping!* Then came the whining sound of a second bullet, passing me and striking the boulder once more.

"Get down! Get down behind a rock or tree!" Turlock bellowed wildly.

I didn't need to be told twice. I dropped Blackie's reins and dove behind the nearest tree, as another bullet pinged against the rock that Mother and Turlock had been standing by.

More scared than I'd ever been in my life, I cried out, "Mother, somebody's shooting at us!"

She shouted back, "Yes. Stay where you are, Fayette. I'm with Mr. Turlock. Eubie! Eubie!"

Over the nickering and stamping of the mules and Hagar, I heard my brother's yell, "I'm okay. I got a tree too!"

I looked to my right, in the direction of his call, and found Eubie crouched down at the base of a huge evergreen ahead of me, but I couldn't see Mother and the Possum. "Mother!" I cried, as a hail of bullets came down onto the rocks and trees behind my boulder. Not just one person was firing at us, but a lot of them. The Gordons? Feuders?

Once more I yelled, "Where are you?"

Turlock answered, "Shut up. Don't draw their fire. She's aw right."

The mules weren't all right, though. Frightened by all the shooting, they were neighing and kicking, rearing on their hind legs, and pawing at the air. All at once the white horse bolted, galloping past me and around Eubie's tree and out of sight. I heard her snort in terror as she sped by. Our riding mules followed her, and after them came the four pack mules with the library saddlebags flapping.

After they'd clattered by, there was quiet except for the spitting of more bullets. When I managed to keep my teeth from chattering long enough to listen, I could hear Turlock's rumbling voice saying, "I can't use the rifle because I can't see anybody to shoot at."

Wherever he and Mother were, they were close to me, because I could hear her clearly, too. "But why would anybody shoot at a librarian?"

"I dunno, but they sure are."

Mother asked my question, "Are they Gordons?"

"Mebbe, but then they'd probably call out their name to let me know who they was."

"Then you think it's somebody else. Maybe bandits?"

"Mebbe. Mebbe they're after the pack mules."

I risked a peek around the side of my tree and saw

both of them now, hunkered down side by side behind a big rock. Turlock had the rifle in his arms but was not aiming it at anyone.

Mother said, "Would people steal books up here?"

He answered her grimly, "They don't know without openin' the saddlebags that they've got books in 'em."

The shooting went on. Sometimes a group of shots came together, then one, followed after a while by another.

I heard Mother say, "Bandits could have caught the library mules by now and taken whatever they wanted off them. Will they come after us, too?"

"More 'n likely. That's when I'll shoot 'em. I'll try to get 'em before they get us, even if there are more of 'em than there are of me."

My heart pounded, thinking of Mother's wedding ring and my locket. Of course, hill-country bandits would want gold things and whatever valuables we had with us.

And to think I was responsible for our situation because of my meddlesomeness and wanting to appear big in the eyes of the rich Hillman girls. As the next bullet hit my tree, I said to myself, "Never, never again."

Suddenly it got quiet, so quiet that I could hear the gurgle of water in the stream. Nobody spoke, waiting, hoping, and praying that the people shooting at us had gone away. Then all at once a man's voice shouted from somewhere ahead on the trail. "Is there a book lady down there dressed up like a man?"

A book lady? A librarian?

Mother called out, "Yes, there is. I'm the librarian

sent up here from Monterey. I have books for Big Tree Junction."

The voice came again. "We caught yer mules. We seen yer books and we can tell you're a woman by yer voice, even if you've got on britches and a man's hat. Who's travelin' with you, lady?"

"My two children."

"We seen some kids with ya. Who's the man?"

"Mr. Turlock!" Mother called back.

There was silence, then amazingly a peal of loud laughter came from a number of men.

A second male voice shouted, "Then you sure ain't no revenue galoots if old Gil's with ya. You're just who the boy here said ya was. Ya can come on out now onto the trail. We won't shoot at ya no more."

I didn't move. What did they mean, 'revenue men'? Who was the boy they were talking about? I looked at the Possum and Mother and saw them leave the shelter of the rock and come back onto the trail. When Eubie joined them, I left my tree too. "What are revenue men?" I asked Mother. "Who was shooting at us?"

The Possum replied, "Moonshiners, men making whiskey in a still. It's aginst the law, so revenue men come up here to catch the moonshiners if they can. Then they throw 'em in jail."

Eubie, whose face was white as snow, asked, "But why would they shoot at us?"

"They thought we was lawmen come to get them. They'll be down here in a bit. Mind how you and yer sis act around 'em."

I asked him, "They know you, Mr. Turlock?"

"Yep, they do seem to, don't they?"

So he had been a moonshine whiskey maker at one time. Otherwise, how would they know him by name and why would they laugh so much when they heard it? He had to be a good friend of theirs.

The moonshiners didn't make us wait long. There were five of them, four tall, youngish ones with beards and one little, clean-shaven older man. He wore a leather coat, while the others were dressed in overalls and plaid flannel shirts. There was another person with them, too, someone wearing a jacket much too big for him, a boy my age with dark-red hair. Joshua Drucker, the orphan boy from the Phipenny homestead. Him here? Why?

He grinned at me and said, "Howdy."

I was speechless with surprise at the sight of him.

"Howdy, Gil," the oldest moonshiner said, nodding to Turlock, and one by one he and the other men shook hands with him. "It's good to see ya back in this part of the hills agin. It's been a long time."

"Yep, nearly eight years by now, I reckon." Turlock's words came in a growl.

The moonshiner took off his hat to Mother and said, "We're sorry to have shot at ya. It was a honest mistake. We haven't got anythin' agin books. The kid here was followin' you folks, and he circled around behind us to tell us who you are. At first, we couldn't believe what he said. But them saddlebags on yer mules proved the truth to us. Revenue men don't carry along a lot of books."

Mother said, as she sat down on a rock, "No, I suppose they don't."

The moonshiner went on. "My boys and me ought to make it up to ya for tryin' to kill ya, so we'd like to visit ya tonight at yer camp with some presents."

Mother looked up at him and said, "Well, sir, I don't know about that."

He added, "We'd invite ya to our camp, but we don't like nobody near our still. Don't ya be scared of us, ma'am. Ya won't come to no harm from any of us. We were plannin' to roast venison for our supper. We'll fetch it to yer camp and cook it there."

Mother looked to the Possum, who nodded at her. "You'll be aw right if they come," he said.

"All right, then come." Mother laughed nervously. "I'll be pleased to invite you all. I don't suppose one of you would be interested in serving as a library outpost for people who come to your camp to buy what you make? After all, library books are being circulated out of the saloon at Pickett's Crossing." Had she lost her mind?

One of the tall young men said, "That's aw right for old man Pickett to do. He stays put. We move around a lot, ma'am. We're pretty hard to find."

Mother laughed again and said she was only making a joke. "Yes, I imagine you do move a good bit, what with revenue agents coming around looking for your still." She seemed to have got her nerve and all of her wits back. "Would you know how we could get a doctor to the Rogers homestead?" she asked suddenly. "They've had typhoid fever there."

The boss nodded and said, "Sure, we'll help. Jake, go to our camp, take one of the horses right away, and ride over to the next valley. I hear tell a travelin' doctor is stayin' there till the end of the week. Catch him and let him know."

"Sure, Pa," Jake agreed.

"Oh, thank heavens we ran into you!" exclaimed Mother.

The old mountaineer added, "Thank the red-headed kid while you're at it. He told us who and what you were. 'Cause of some book of yers. He's been trailin' ya for days now."

"A book?" asked Mother, staring at Joshua Drucker.

"Sure." Joshua reached into the deep side pocket of the big old coat he wore and pulled out a book. I knew it at once. Edgar Allan Poe was back with us!

Joshua said, "I guess you must'a forgotten this book when you rode away from the homestead. I found it under the porch, and I might'a kept it, but the words in it were mostly too big for me to read. Figurin' that with the bad welcome ya got at my place ya wouldn't ever be back, I decided to come after ya and bring yer book to ya. Keepin' it if I couldn't read it would have been like stealin'. I thought mebbe I could help ya out with the camp chores. Ya don't have to pay me, and I don't eat much."

He handed the book to Mother as the mountaineers clustered around. "What I'm sayin' is that I've run off to go to work for sombody I like better than those folks I was with. They won't care much, not enough to come after me. Besides, I'm almost of an age to be out on my own anyhow. I'm almost sixteen."

134

Suddenly Joshua thought of something else. "Oh, ma'am, I brought ya a present." He opened his coat to show us a pistol in his belt. It was a very large, long-barrelled one. As he drew it out and handed it, butt end first, to Mother, he said, "It's a horse pistol that belonged to Mr. Pickett's pa, who used it in the Civil War. I traded four wolf pelts I cured for it at Pickett's Crossing last month. Mr. Pickett nailed 'em up on the walls of his saloon. I want ya to have the pistol for lettin' me travel with ya. It'll be some payment for what ya feed me."

"Good heavens!" Mother exclaimed, as she sat on her rock with Edgar Allan Poe in her left hand and a horse pistol in her right. I'd never seen her look so surprised.

I went wearily over to sit down next to her, leaving the five moonshiners, Joshua Drucker, the Possum, and Eubie talking together in a friendly fashion.

For quite a while Mother was silent. Then she said, as if to herself, "Well, it seems we're to have guests tonight. I wonder what it will be like to be entertained by moonshiners?"

"I doubt if it'll be dull, Mother," I answered.

Soon the boss came over to us and said, "Aw right, ma'am, we'll take ya to a good camping spot. We've got yer animals tied a ways up the trail, and we'll bring 'em back now. My boy Jake'll head out for the doctor right off. We'll make yer camp for ya, so y'all can get some rest before supper. You're a mite pasty-faced, and so's yer little gal. We'll plan to leave ya a gift of some tobacco and whiskey to cheer ya up."

Mother told him, "I do not drink or smoke, Mr. — I'm sorry, but I don't know your name. I didn't catch it."

"I never said it, that's why. I don't ever aim to tell ya what it is, ma'am. We don't go by last names in these parts. We know ya probably don't chew or smoke. The tobacco's for the mules. They like it. The whiskey'll be our best. It's my pride and joy." He grinned at us.

Mother said, "We already have some whiskey for the mare. It used to belong to Mr. Denver Murfree. We were told that the horse likes it in her feed sometimes."

The mountaineer chuckled. "Yep, a horse sometimes does. Well, given that Gil Turlock is yer mule skinner, I reckon that whiskey is all gone by now, so you'll need a new supply." He didn't wait for Mother to say anything but walked away to join the other men.

As Mother got up, she said, "Fayette, what could he have meant by that remark? I've been told that Mr. Turlock does not drink. He has not touched the whiskey in the saddlebags. I saw it when I looked for books the last time."

I told her, "People have told you a lot of things, Mother!"

"Indeed they have, Fayette," she said, as she handed the hoodoo book back to me and stuffed the old pistol into the belt that held up her riding breeches.

One thing I could surely say for the moonshiners was that they were dead set on treating us well after shooting at us. All of them but Jake, who went for the doctor, es-

136

corted us to a nice flowery meadow for our campsite that night. Turlock walked with them and Eubie with Joshua, but Mother and I rode our mules. I hadn't really wanted to ride when our mules were brought back to us, but a tall young moonshiner jerked me off my feet and dumped me like a sack of oats into the saddle after he'd done the same for Mother.

The men set up our ladies' tent first of all and stood waiting and grinning till Mother and I went inside it.

I asked her, "What are we supposed to do in here?"

"I don't know, Fayette, but I think it would be wise not to go out till they call us." As she spoke, she took the pistol out of her belt and set it on the floor of the tent. "Good heavens, that thing's heavy! I can barely move my knee when I walk. Do you suppose it's loaded?"

"I think so, don't you?"

Mother got down onto her knees and began to unroll her sleeping bag. "I suspect so. But at times I don't know what I do know anymore, Fayette. I can only take one day at a time up here. I never know what's next. Who would have dreamed being a librarian could be so strenuous? But I can't say Mr. Wallace didn't warn me."

I said glumly, "Mr. Wallace and Mr. Embleton too must have known about moonshiners. Maybe the mountains really aren't any place for a lady."

Mother sat back on her heels. "Fayette, don't say that, please! We're not far now from Big Tree Junction. We've got the library's books this far. Don't make me lose heart. Somehow we'll get them all the way to the desperate ladies who want them."

The desperate ladies? Well, I knew two more ladies who were lots more desperate at this moment than the five in Big Tree Junction.

I asked, "How shall we act tonight, Mother?"

"Politely and naturally. Be ladylike. Be gracious." She nodded as she lay down on top of her sleeping bag. "We shall eat venison, accept the tobacco and the whiskey for Hagar, and I shall give the men a going-away gift. A book."

I was pretty sure that it wouldn't be the Poe book, but still I tried to suggest it. "Maybe one of them is a good enough reader for the book Joshua brought back."

"No, not Poe. I think a volume of stories from the Bible would be best, one with pictures in it they can ponder if they have the time and inclination."

I didn't say anything. Instead, I unrolled my sleeping bag too and lay down beside her, listening to the men as they set up the camp. She told me to listen for Eubie's voice, which was the highest one, to make sure he was all right. I heard him lots of times as the day wore on.

As twilight came, the voices got louder and louder, and Mother said in the gloom of our tent, "What I was afraid of has happened!"

"What's that?"

"They've sent back to their camp for the presents for our horse and have brought some cheer for themselves."

"What cheer?"

"Their whiskey."

"Oh."

After a time, Eubie stuck his head into the tent to tell us to come out and "grub up," which meant that supper was ready. He looked to me as if he'd had a good time that afternoon. He would!

"Courage, Fayette! Keep your nerve up," Mother told me, as we came out together.

There around the fire stood all of the whiskey makers, including Jake who had returned, Joshua, and Turlock. Each of the five moonshiners had a tin cup in his hand. The boss lifted his to Mother and said, "Here's to ya, ma'am." Then he and the other men drank.

One man shouted, "Here's to the pretty little lady," and they all lifted their cups to me.

Me? They thought I was pretty.

Eubie cried, "Mother, Fayette, come and eat!" and he pointed to a fallen tree that we could sit on. Beside it a haunch of deer meat was being roasted over a fire.

The boss said, "I'll serve the womenfolks." He piled our plates with beans and corn bread and chunks of venison and then brought them over to us. Though he wasn't too steady on his feet and I was scared he'd dump my plate on my lap, I didn't warn him to be careful but only muttered, "Thank you, mister."

After we started to eat, the men filled their plates and began to eat too. At the same time, they continued to drink from one of the big glass jugs set on the ground beside the fire.

All at once Jake put down the banjo he'd been plunking away at and said very loudly, "Hey, it don't appear to me that our friend Gil Turlock's doin' any drinkin'. That don't seem very polite to my way of thinkin'."

The Possum told him, "I don't hanker for whiskey tonight, Jake."

A second moonshiner took up Jake's teasing. "It's an insult to our moonshine not to drink any. Mebbe we ought to offer some of it to the book lady."

"No, thank you," Mother told him firmly.

Turlock added, "She don't want any of yer moonshine!"

"And you don't seem to neither, Gil," accused Jake. "Do you think it's got poison in it? You better have a cup with us, Turlock."

The boss laughed and said, "Gil, to keep the peace you better do what Jake says. This boy can get a bad nature when he hears No said more'n once to him in a single night."

I felt Mother's hand on my knee, warning me to be still, and I tensed, feeling her stiffen beside me on the log.

Turlock growled, "Aw right. I'll have a cup then." I saw him get up and lumber over to the jug, pour himself a drink from it, and return to the place where he'd been sitting. Afterward, Jake went back to playing on his banjo, picking out a tune I didn't know.

Mother got up now, stretched, and said over the banjo, "My daughter and I will be happy to wash up after all of you if you will give us your plates and cups."

The boss chuckled and told her, "The boys here can do the plates at the creek over yonder." He pointed to Eubie and Joshua. "But only the plates, mind ya, kids. We'll be keepin' the cups with us. You womenfolks stay where ya are. Just sit on yer log and look pretty."

Eubie and Joshua came over together to get our

plates, and Mother whispered, "Boys, please be very careful. Do what they tell you to."

She sat down again, and after a while she said to the mountaineers, "I have a gift for you gentlemen as a thank-you present for such a fine supper. It's a very nice book I think you might enjoy, one with uplifting pictures."

"Pictures of what?" asked Jake, stopping the music.

"Stories from the Bible. I'd like to give it to you from the Monterey library, and then, if you don't mind, my daughter and I are very weary and would like to retire for the night to our tent."

After a long silence, the boss said, "That's mighty kind of ya, ma'am, to give us a book. We'll leave ya the tobacco plugs and the extra jug of whiskey, when we're done with the first jug here."

"Fine," agreed Mother. "I'll get the book right now. It's in a saddlebag on the smallest mule. I can see quite clearly where you've put it." She left me and went over to the pile of things that had been unpacked.

Alone on the log by the fire, I kept very quiet, watching the men and Turlock, who was drinking with them. I wished Eubie and Joshua would come back. I felt very lonesome sitting there all by myself.

Mother found the book fast, a big black-bound one, and came back holding it to her chest. She went over to the boss and handed it to him with the words, "This is not being loaned to you. It's a gift! You won't be expected to return it to me or to the library down in Monerey. It is yours to keep."

141

"Thank you kindly, ma'am. It isn't everyday somebody gifts us with a book." He tucked it under his arm where he sat. "In fact, it never has happened to me in my whole life before."

Mother said, "I hope you will enjoy it." She turned to call to me as Jake started in on the banjo again. "Come, Fayette, we'll be saying good-night now to these gentlemen." She added to the Possum, "Will you please tell my son and Joshua that I expect them to go directly to bed once they've come back here? I see the other tent is ready for them."

"Sure enough. I'll tell 'em for ya." I caught the Possum's eyes with mine as I passed him on my way to our tent. He was looking at me over the rim of his cup. Suddenly he rose to his feet and went over to the open jug of whiskey by the fire.

Inside the tent with Mother, listening to Jake play the banjo, I whispered, "The Possum's gone back to the whiskey just now."

A deep, sorrowful sigh came from her.

"Mother, what'll we do?"

"Stay in here and pray that nobody gets the idea he wants to dance with a lady from Monterey."

"What if he does?"

"Then we go out and dance, Fayette."

I could dance the two-step and the waltz but had no idea what moonshine makers danced up in the hills. Here was another thing that *Heidi* had not prepared me for. As a matter of fact, reading that book hadn't prepared me for much at all in these mountains.

Mother and I sat in the dark together, listening. When we heard Eubie's voice speaking to Joshua in the tent on the other side of us, she sighed with relief. "The Lord be praised," she said. "The boys are safely out of the way too. Turlock gave them my message."

"Maybe going inside was Joshua's idea," I told her. I doubted if Eubie would have that much good sense. He looked as if he had been having a good time with the moonshiners in spite of the fact that a couple of hours ago they'd been trying to shoot us. Then I asked her, "Mother, what are we going to do with Joshua Drucker?"

"Keep him with us, I suppose. Who knows what might happen to him if he went back to the homestead he ran away from? We can't cast him adrift alone in these hills. I am sure he can find work to his liking in Big Tree Junction. We can ask the desperate ladies to help him."

"I hope they can." I thought for a bit about him. "We ought to be very grateful to him for what he did, telling the moonshiners who we were."

"I *am* grateful, Fayette. He probably saved our lives."

"But, Mother, he sure did bring you a queer present."

Mother laughed sharply. "Yes, the pistol is odd, isn't it? And I wonder why that rather difficult Poe book was left behind at the Phipenny homestead as a present."

I had planned what I'd say to cover up my leaving the book. "Oh, I did that! I was sitting on the porch, reading it, and I left it."

"Fayette, I can't recall ever seeing you sitting on the

143

porch there," she said. "You should not give library property to anyone!"

I was embarrassed. "Well, I'm sorry, but it turned out to be for just a little while, didn't it? You know how I like porches." I would have rattled on and on about porches, because I was getting more and more nervous, but I stopped because the banjo playing had stopped.

Outside the men's voices by the fire had been getting louder and louder, and now they were shouting at each other. What were they doing? All of them were yelling, calling out names mostly. "Jake!" "Roscoe!" Over all the noise I could hear our mules braying.

I asked Mother, "Should I peek outside?"

"No, I will."

She passed in front of me, parted the closed tent flap, and looked out. Then she gasped. "Oh, oh, my Lord!"

I crawled to the edge of the tent, lifted up a side, and looked out too.

Oh, what a fight was going on by the fire! The whiskey makers were fighting each other and Turlock, too. A war seemed to be going on out there. Every time a man got knocked down by another, up he got and hit the man who was standing next to him. Sometimes that man fell over. Sometimes he kept on his feet and hit back. The Possum, bigger even than Jake, was in the thick of it. I saw two moonshiners jump on his back, but they didn't pull him down. He shrugged them off, and when they came back at him from the front, he punched them both and knocked them down. Then he pulled them up by their overall straps and bashed their heads together,

144

making a thudding sound. Next another big mountaineer came at Turlock, who hit him so hard under the chin that he sailed through the air and fell over the log I'd been sitting on.

By this time only two moonshiners were still upright, a red-bearded one and the boss. The red-bearded one tackled Turlock, who at once kicked him away. Heavily he fell next to the other one at the log.

Then the boss yelled, "That's enough fun, Gil! Me and the boys'll go home now. We sure had a fine evenin' here with you and the womenfolks. Come on, boys." He walked to the other men and prodded each one with the toe of his boot until he got up. Some of the moonshiners had eyes that were going to blacken, and one had a bleeding nose that he wiped with his shirt sleeve.

Once they were all on their feet, the boss said, "We'll leave the little book lady her own whiskey jug and what's left in the other one for Turlock here to finish. Let's get our rifles and horses and make our farewells." He chuckled. "Turlock, you ain't changed one bit over the years. So long. I'm glad we didn' shoot ya today by mistake, but we never did expect to see ya back here, given what happened to ya."

I saw the five of them walk out of the circle of the campfire and over to their tethered horses at the meadow's edge. Alone, the Possum swayed from side to side, standing next to the dying campfire. A huge black silhouette, he looked more like a bear than ever. Suddenly he moved, going toward the two whiskey jugs beside the blaze.

145

Explosively Mother said one word, "No!" Then she whispered, "Fayette, get out of here! Circle around to where Turlock keeps his bedroll and Murfree's rifle. Get the rifle and take it with you into the trees. Hide it and yourself."

"*Me?*"

"Yes, you! Hurry! I've got the tent flap open for you."

I scooted past her, my heart beating fast. I thought it might jump out of my chest. One glance at the Possum showed that his attention was on the whiskey, not on our tents. I scrambled on my hands and knees between our tent and Eubie's. Then, bending over, I hurried behind the tents to where I'd seen Turlock's gear earlier that night. Yes, there it was—Denver Murfree's rifle, leaning against a tree. I grabbed hold of it, slid behind the tree, and, moving as quickly and as quietly as I could, went deeper into the grove of trees beside the camp.

What was Mother going to do? What was I to do now that I had the rifle?

I saw her come out into the firelight with that big old horse pistol in both of her hands, aiming at Turlock. Her voice rang out. "Mr. Turlock, you get away from that whiskey jug! I know about you and what you did eight years ago. I heard that you claimed then that it happened because of whiskey, and I believe it too. I saw you fighting just now. I did not find it amusing, even if the moonshiners did. Someone could have been badly hurt. Of all people, you ought to know that! Pick up your bedroll. Then you get out of this camp and out of our lives right now!"

146

I held my breath as he turned around, tin cup in hand, to gape at Mother. All he said was, "Ma'am?"

Would he attack her? Would she shoot him? Could she shoot him? Would I have to shoot him then? I raised the rifle to my shoulder and put my finger into the trigger like a cowboy in the movies. Oh, how the rifle shook! How heavy it was! It got heavier by the second.

I gritted my teeth. Yes, I'd shoot him if he attacked Mother. I looked down the rifle barrel through the sights, making ready and praying.

There was a long, long moment while the two of them looked at other. Finally he shouted a queer thing, "A pet wolf keeps coyotes away!"

All at once he threw the whiskey from the cup into the fire, making the flame blaze up high for an instant. Then he turned away from Mother, walking fast toward his bedroll. I saw him pick it up, throw it over his shoulder, and pass not twenty feet from me as he went into the trees byond the camp.

Lord be praised! Glory be! Hallelujah! Mother had won! The Terrible Turlock was out of our lives. Him and his moonshine drinking. Him and his whistling to birds and scaring our mules by just looking at them. Him and his scowling and growling. Him and his talking about the whites of my eyes and about pet wolves and coyotes. But then what was he but a wild man of the woods anyhow? Didn't he realize it was 1916?

Lowering the rifle, I came out of the trees and walked up to my mother, who had to be the bravest librarian in the world.

147

She let the horse pistol fall to waist level, though she still held it in both hands, and said, "Fayette, I think I might faint!"

I told her, "I'd like to faint too, but I don't think we'd better. We should keep guard here all night. Come over and sit down on the log with me. If I don't sit soon, I'll fall, I'm trembling so much."

7

Eubie and Joshua came out of their tent only seconds after Mother and I had sat down together. Eubie demanded, "What happened?" He looked around. "Where's the Possum? We heard him talking about a wolf! Where's the wolf?"

Mother said, "Mr. Turlock has left the employ of the library. I saw that he was getting drunk." She took a deep breath, then went on, staring into the flames of the campfire.

"Of all men, Turlock should not drink. He cannot deal with alcohol. It poisons him, and he loses control when he drinks. Some people are affected that way. The last time he drank heavily was years ago, as I heard it, and something horrible happened. He killed his wife's brother in a fistfight."

Mother looked sadly at us. "Mr. Mackenzie told me what he knew of his story. After the fight, Turlock had no memory of killing his brother-in-law at all. The United States marshal came to the settlement where he lived, which was not far from Big Tree Junction, and took him down out of the hills for a trial. He was found guilty and sent to prison for some years on a charge of manslaughter. When he was released, he returned to the

149

mountains and became a sort of hermit. I have no idea why he wants to go to Big Tree Junction at this point or what could bring him into any feud."

She put the huge pistol across her knees and said, "He was defended in court by, of all people, Mr. Herbert, who lost his case. I remembered when I met Turlock that I had once heard your father talk of the mountaineer who was a peaceful giant but went completely crazy when he drank. Mr. Herbert thought him a wild beast. So that is why I drove Turlock away before he could harm any one of us."

"Oh, my!" was all I could say, as I thought of Mrs. Pickett's warning to me. So this horrible thing is what she'd meant by "doing it again."

I said, "You did the right thing, Mother."

She was looking at me as she said, "Fayette, I didn't tell you and Eubie about Turlock's past, because I didn't want to frighten you. I gambled on his staying sober to get us to Big Tree Junction, and I lost my gamble. Now here we sit, stranded in the middle of nowhere with no muleteer. Mr. Turlock won't return, I know. He doesn't need us. He can live very well alone in the hills and can make his own way to Big Tree Junction. We wouldn't be able to find the moonshiners and get aid from them, because they are moving their camp. I'm frankly afraid of firing the rifle as a signal to attract attention, because I'm afraid of who might come here."

For the first time, Joshua Drucker spoke up. "Ma'am, you're sure right about that." He looked worried too. "Who was the Possum supposed to be feudin' with?" he asked.

150

I told him, "The Gordons."

He nodded. "I heard of them. They're a whole tribe up here. With Turlock gone, you needn't worry about them folks, though."

I asked Mother, "What are we going to do?"

"At this moment, I do not know, Fayette."

"Well, I know," piped up Eubie. "We'll go on to Big Tree Junction."

"Wherever that is," said Mother gloomily.

Joshua spoke softly, "I think I know the direction. Eubie told me he can handle the mules."

I exclaimed, "*Eubie?*"

"Sure, Fayette. I listened hard to Mr. Murfree and watched him and the Possum close. I can do it. I can pack Hagar," bragged my brother. Then he asked Mother, "Should I kick over the whiskey jugs for you, or do you and Fayette plan to shoot 'em?"

"Kick them over, Eubie. Then you and Joshua go back to your tent. You, too, Fayette. I'll keep watch out here."

I said, "I'll keep it with you, Mother."

"All right. Thank you."

We sat together and watched Eubie kick over one whiskey jug, pour the contents of the second one onto the ground, and then go off with Joshua to the tent.

Mother and I didn't speak again till dawn. Then, as an owl hooted nearby, she said, "I surely pray that Eubie can do what he says he can!"

I wanted to say "Don't count on it," but didn't. After all he was only ten years old. So I sat and thought of my dark secrets and Mother's, of the Terrible Turlock, and

151

about tomorrow morning. I just knew it was going to be awful.

Awful wasn't the right word. It was dreadful, a morning worthy of Mr. Edgar Allan Poe.

As he said, Eubie had listened to Denver Murfree and watched the Possum with the mules and mare, but he didn't handle them the same way. He cussed them out at the top of his lungs, using the words Mr. Murfree had whispered. Mother didn't like his method, I did not like it, and the mules didn't like it either. They fought having their bridles and saddles and library saddlebags put on their backs. They kicked and plunged. Old Noah was a terror on four feet, trying to bite and kick Joshua, who was hard put to dodge his teeth and lashing hooves. The only animal that behaved at all well was Hagar, who let Joshua stow the tents and our other gear on her back the way Eubie told him to.

"Thank God for Hagar," said Mother, when we were at last ready to break camp.

We set out with Joshua on Bruno, who didn't take to him and kept bucking until Eubie cussed him into decent behavior. Then came Hagar as usual, Eubie on Ishmael next to her, Noah, Shem, Ham, Japheth, Mother astride Brownie, and me on Blackie. The lineup of people and animals was the same.

Yet it was different. The mules knew it was. They were jittery, switching their big ears around to catch any wilderness noise they could shy at. Blackie was plenty nervous, jerking his head up and twitching his muscles all the time. I was just as jumpy as he was. Not having had any sleep the night before didn't help my nerves one bit. I was glad the Terrible Turlock was out of our lives so I wouldn't have to worry about him, but all the same traveling with him as our mule skinner had been quieter and more peaceful than with Eubie.

The oldest mule, Noah, seemed to rejoice that things had changed. As we left, he even tried to take a chunk out of Hagar, who gave him a good, solid kick in the brisket.

That night was as dreadful as the day. We had troubles getting the mules unloaded and unsaddled and then hobbled so they wouldn't stray. I had to help and was nearly stepped on twice. We ate a cold supper, because it began to rain too hard to start a fire.

The next morning our troubles truly hit us. Our one friend among the animals was sick, still standing up but shuddering with her head drooping low. Hagar was in a bad way.

"What'll we do?" asked Eubie, almost in tears.

Mother stood in the clearing where everything green dripped water from last night's downpour. It was still drizzling now. "We coped with Mr. Murfree's foot with a book and coped with the funeral with books. I bet Mr. Wallace put a book on veterinary medicine in our saddlebags. Children, let's look for it. We shall try to consider this as another reference question and keep our nerve."

We'd piled the library's saddlebags under a tree to try to keep them dry, but all the same they were glistening with rain and stiff from cold. Working separately, we unbuckled bags, and, of course, I ran across the hoodoo book packed next to the bottle of Mr. Murfree's whiskey. I refused to touch it but dug to the very bottom of the bag, and there I found a book on animal diseases. A big book, it covered cows, sheep, pigs, donkeys, mules, and horses, glory be. It had 600 pages of diseases in it, and I marveled at it.

Mother took the book from me and went back to our tent, where we all sat down while she went through it. Frowning, she muttered to herself about warbles, glanders, and spavins, all horse ailments. At last she said, "Ah, I think I have it now! This must be what Hagar has." And she read off a long name.

I asked, "Can we save her?" I knew as well as anybody else that we couldn't go on without Hagar nor could we return without her. If she didn't budge, neither would the eight mules.

Mother nodded. "We can try to save her. We must get her inside out of the rain."

Eubie said, "But she's too big for a tent."

"Not for two tents, Eubie. We'll move one tent against the other and open up the rear and front ends to make one big one out of the two. It will hold the mare and us, too. The book says to get her inside, curry her and keep her warm."

Working together, we lined up the two tents and, with Eubie leading her, got Hagar inside. Naturally, all of the mules followed behind her, clustering in front of the tent door and staring at what went on. Eubie and Joshua curried the shivering horse, and then I put a blanket over her back. But she went on shivering and hanging her head.

Then I remembered what Mother had told us about Hagar while we were at the Mackenzie homestead. "Mother", I asked, "have we still got rolled oats?" We'd had porridge twice for breakfast.

"Why, yes, I believe we do. We haven't used all of it."

I went out, rummaged in the supply bags, and found the round, cardboard package of oats. Then I went to the saddlebag I'd seen the hoodoo book in, got the whiskey out, and hurried to the tent with a long-handled skillet we used to cook with.

I opened the oat box, filled the skillet almost to the top with oats, then poured the whiskey over the oats.

Hagar nickered. An instant later her head came up to the skillet, her nostrils snuffling. Then she shot out her lips and began to eat the whiskey-soaked oats.

I said, "Malindy was right. We did have a use for the whiskey!"

"Give her some more," suggested Eubie. "She's perking up."

So I fixed another half skillet of oats and whiskey, and Hagar ate up every bit. Then, all at once, she sank down onto her knees.

"Grab the tent pole next to you, Joshua!" ordered Mother.

He got it just before the mare rolled over on her side with a deep, wheezing sound. Planting the pole at one side of her head, he fixed the tent so it stayed up. Eubie bent over the mare, listened to her breathing, and put his hand on her. "She's resting now and isn't shivering anymore. I guess she doesn't hurt anywhere."

Mother told us all, "I doubt that she does hurt. She's

had all the oats and two-thirds of the whiskey. I think Hagar will rest for a time. She's had a goodly number of nips, enough to kill anything but a horse."

Eubie said, "I'll sit down and hold her head in my lap after I go out and tell Ishmael that his ma's all right."

Mother surprised me by laughing."Eubie, you do that! Tell all of the mules that we aren't licked yet. We'll keep Hagar company and take turns holding her head."

Just at dawn, while Eubie was tending her and I was trying to sleep, I heard him cry, "Look out! She's rising!" I rolled over fast to the edge of the tent and looked up. Hagar was standing, tossing her head and shaking herself the way a dog does when he gets wet. I watched her walk to the door of the tent, which Joshua leaped to open up for her, and step out into the sunshine. What a loud braying welcome she got from our eight mules! How they doted on her!

She was all right after her oats-and-whiskey treatment, and after our breakfast we got her and the mules ready to go in our usual line of travel. But for all his cussing, including some bad words I had never heard once on the schoolgrounds back home, Eubie couldn't manage the mules. Noah was more full of the devil than ever, trying to make mischief whenever he could. I could tell from the back of the line that Noah was up to no good by the way he kept twitching his moth-eaten tail in circles as he went along behind Hagar.

That mule got his chance at trouble that very afternoon as we went along a ledge with a sloping ravine to the right and a cliff to the left. I saw old Noah drop a distance behind Hagar until Shem, who followed him with his head hanging, was just on his heels. Then all at once Noah laid back his ears and flashed out with his hind legs, catching Shem by surprise.

Shem jumped backward to the right, lost his footing on the pebbly trail, let out a loud, scared bray, and slid over the edge of the ravine, disappearing into it.

Mother yelled, "Joshua, stop! Shem's gone down the mountain!"

I saw Joshua turn around in the saddle, look back onto the trail, and then continue to ride over the ledge to wider ground where it was safe. We followed him there and dismounted.

Mother's face was pasty white. "I've got to go down there to the mule."

"I'll go," volunteered Joshua.

"No, it's my responsibility. This is library business. The library books are in the saddlebags. I have to see to the mule and then to the books. Please get me some rope from Hagar's pack, and tie it to a tree trunk. I'll take the pistol down with me. That poor animal is surely dying, if not dead."

"Sure, ma'am."

Eubie asked, "Are you going to shoot Shem, Mother?"

"If I have to, I will." She sounded very grim. "I surely can't leave him there to starve with a broken back or legs!" What a look she gave to Noah. "There is an animal I would not mind shooting if he belonged to me."

I'd never seen Mother act this way before. The mountains had changed her. Life was hard up here. No wonder Mr. Embleton had not wanted to come to the hills.

Joshua tied a long rope to a tree near the edge of the ravine. With the pistol in her belt, Mother took hold of the rope and backed to the rim of the ledge. Then she stepped down over the edge and was out of sight.

I went out onto the ledge, lay face down on it, and looked over into the ravine. But I could not see her or Shem because of all the underbrush growing down in it and along the sides. At least, if Mother lost hold of the rope, she'd have something to grab onto.

Joshua and Eubie stood behind me with the animals, Joshua holding the rifle.

How quiet it was, so quiet I could hear my heart beating. There was no noise from the ravine or ahead of me on the trail, not even a bird sound. Then all at once I heard the sound of footsteps coming crunching over the pebbly ground along the ledge. Joshua? Eubie? I twisted my head to look at the boys and saw that Joshua had raised the rifle to his shoulder and was taking aim. Eubie stood open-mouthed beside him. Turning my head, I looked in the other direction, to the other end of the ledge, and there to my horror stood the Terrible Turlock. Him *here? Now?* With Mother down in the ravine and us all alone?

Speechless with fright, I watched him, waiting for him *to cross* the ledge. If he did, he'd have to step on me first. I rolled over and got to my feet, ready to run back to Eubie and Joshua.

Just as I reached my feet I saw Turlock open his big

leather coat with both hands. The glint of metal shone at his waistline. There was a pistol in his belt. He didn't reach toward it; he only stood there, at the end of the ledge, holding his coat open with both hands.

I caught my breath, understanding something. He could have shot any one of us at any time! He'd probably had the pistol ever since we'd first seen him at the Mackenzie homestead. When Mother had driven him off, he was armed and could easily have fired on us from outside our camp. But he had not, not even when he was drunk.

I screamed to Joshua, "Don't shoot him! We need him!" I pointed toward the ravine and called to Turlock. "Mother's down there with Shem! He fell."

"I saw it," he shouted back. Then he came along the ledge and stood towering over me. "I figgered sooner or later somethin' like this would happen. I wanted to tell ya too that the boy here took the wrong trail for Big Tree Junction when ya set out this morning."

I asked, "Oh, please, we're in awful trouble. Can't you help Mother?"

"Mebbe so. I'll go down and take a look at what's below." He took hold of the rope, swung over the ravine's edge, and down he went along the rope.

A cold sweat came out all over me. Mother didn't know the Possum was back and that he didn't mean us any harm. She might shoot him when he showed up below. I hesitated for a few seconds; then I caught hold of the rope too and slid over the brink. As I went down the slanting sides, I yelled, "Mother, don't shoot anybody! Don't shoot at all!"

159

I'd never gone down a rope before. How it burned my hands, though I tried as hard as I could to put my weight on my feet, not on my arm. My boot soles slipped a lot on rocks, and the bushes I kept bumping into as I descended weren't half as feathery and soft as they looked from the top.

Finally I reached the bottom, dropping three or so feet where the rope ended. I landed with a yell. "Don't shoot the Possum, Mother!"

He was there, standing a short distance away, looking at me and closing his coat again. "Come on, sis, let's find your ma and the mule. You call her for me. We'll track her by her voice."

"Mother, Mother!" I shouted. "Where are you?"

"Over here with Shem!" came a shout from our right.

Turlock went ahead to push tree branches and brush out of the way. "What'd you mean the other night," I asked him, "when you said, 'A pet wolf keeps coyotes away,' Mr. Turlock?"

He told me, "It's a old saying. I was your pet wolf. If I hadn't been with ya, them coyote moonshiners would'a made yer mother drink with 'em and maybe you and your brother too."

"Oh?" What an unpleasant thought. Feeling ashamed of my suspicion, I said, "Yes, Mother was scared they might do that. Will you shoot the mule for her?"

"If I got to, I will. But don't be hasty."

We soon found Mother and Shem. The library saddlebags were lying on the ground, but Shem was not. To my amazement, he was standing up, chewing on the twigs of a small tree. Shem was skinned and bleeding all along one side but otherwise looked all right. Yet he must have fallen two hundred and fifty feet, at least!

Turlock said, "It's hard to kill a mule." He nodded to Mother. "I'm back, ma'am. I won't ever drink agin and upset ya. It wasn't my idea the other night, remember?"

I saw how doubtful Mother looked and, standing behind Turlock, I nodded frantically at her. Finally, she said, "Yes. Now will you please shoot this poor animal for me? Eventually, Shem will run out of food down here. There's nothing on the other side of this ravine but a sheer rock face to a stream below. I cannot leave him here to starve after we get the library books up with the rope."

The Possum did a queer thing. He chuckled. "Why, ma'am, we'll get the books *and* him up to the top too!"

"Could you? Could you save Shem?" Mother sounded as if she didn't believe him and might cry at any minute. I know my eyes had filled with tears.

"I think we can get him up if all of us haul." The Possum turned to me. "Sis, go back up to the trail and ask the boys to give ya all the rope they can get out of Hagar's pack. Then you come back down here with it."

"Please do as he says, Fayette," ordered Mother.

So up I went and astonished Joshua and Eubie with the news that Shem was alive and "almost" all right. I came down with two coils of rope wound about my shoulders. Mr. Murfree sure believed in having lots of rope along, and I found myself blessing him for it now. Back in the bottom of the ravine, I watched Turlock

161

with wonder as he knotted ropes to make a sort of belly-shoulder sling for the mule, fitting it on him and attaching two ropes to it at the top of the mule's back.

Then he said, "I'll go and set things out above to haul up this animal. The saddlebags can go up on the first rope later on. That'll be the easy part. Ma'am, you and yer girl stay down here and keep Shem comp'ny until I yell for the two of ya to come up."

Quickly he went up the first rope with the two long ropes tied to the mule's sling looped over his big shoulder. While we waited below, I told Mother about the pet wolf and coyote business. Hearing the explanation made her sigh and sit down on a rock near Shem, who was eating on a bush.

Pretty soon we heard a yell from Turlock, and then he shouted down over the edge, "You'll be needed to haul, so you better come up now."

Mother said to me, "He left the two of us down here deliberately, Fayette, so we could talk about him. Shem doesn't need our company."

I said, "Yes, I guess he did." Again I felt ashamed of all my suspicions.

She and I went up the rope and at the top found Eubie and Joshua beside two stout pine trees that were growing close together across the ledge. Both trees were wound about with ropes, which led down to Shem in the ravine.

Mr. Turlock showed us what he wanted us to do. He grabbed hold of one rope and told Mother, Eubie, Joshua, and me to grab hold of the other and "pull hard as we could."

"Don't let go! We can do it even if he weighs five hundred pounds. The trees'll take most of his weight on the way up."

I grabbed hold of our rope behind Eubie, dug my heels in, and pulled as hard as I could. I could feel my arms take the strain of the mule's weight and thought they would spring from their sockets, but I went on pulling. Pretty soon a quarter ton of braying, struggling mule began to rise in his sling, sliding along the slope of the ravine. He was coming up all right. The length of rope toiling behind us was getting longer and longer, and I could see that the Possum had a lot of rope behind him too. What a tug-of-war player he would be. Glory be, we were doing it!

The first we saw of Shem was the top of his long ears over the edge. Then came his head with his eyes rolling and gradually the rest of him, until he lay thrashing, kicking, and making mule noises on the ledge. When we let our ropes go slack on Turlock's order, Shem got up at once and walked, trailing his lines, to where the other mules were standing. He was all right. Openmouthed, I watched him go over to old Noah, who was grazing on some moss, kick him hard in the side, then return to Hagar to stand muzzle to muzzle with her as if to tell her all about his dreadful adventure. Clearly Shem knew a foe from a friend, which was something I had not figured out with the Possum. No wonder people talked about mule sense!

A half hour later Turlock had the saddlebags up out of the ravine and onto Shem, who had been doctored with liniment poured over his skinned-up hide and given some tobacco to eat. Then, with Joshua mounted double with Eubie on Ishmael, we were on our way to Big Tree Junction back across the ledge again. Joshua had been taking us to the ocean. Not until we were over the ledge entirely did the thought come to me that "The Fall of the House of Usher" had been in one of Shem's saddlebags right next to what had been left of Mr. Murfree's whiskey. Even if mules were very durable, glass bottles weren't. For sure, the whiskey bottle would have smashed and drenched the hoodoo book. I'd never get rid of it now with a stained cover and smelling of whiskey. It would probably go back to Monterey with us and give us more bad luck.

That night we slept under some old oaks beside a pretty lake, the nicest campsite we'd had yet. We had a good dinner, too. Because he must have sensed that we truly trusted him now, Mr. Turlock kept his promise to bring us some wild food from the hills. He went into the woods around the lake and came back with some green, feathery stuff and half a hatful of wild mushrooms. Then he cooked all of the stuff together in a skillet of bacon fat, and it was really good!

After we'd eaten, he told us, "We'll be comin' into Big Tree Junction tomorrow."

"Are we that close to it?" asked Mother.

"Yes, we are, ma'am." He didn't speak happily.

I began to wonder about him. He'd come from somewhere around Big Tree Junction, so the Gordons must live nearby. What would happen to him up here? Would Big Tree Junction be the end of the trail for him, even though it was only halfway for us? I also thought about Joshua Drucker. What would happen to him here? Would the Phipennys have guessed he'd joined us and send somebody to the town after him? I couldn't say that I knew Joshua well, but he'd been a good friend to us even if he wasn't a good guide, and I hoped he would be happy from now on.

The next day, in the middle of the afternoon, we came into Big Tree Junction. We didn't gallop; we didn't even trot. We walked as we'd done all along, and though I knew he ached to, Eubie didn't blow his trumpet.

I could see right off how Big Tree Junction got its name. There stood a huge pine tree in a clear space, and around it was the town—ten houses, a saloon, and a post office. None of the wooden houses was painted. The only paint that I could see was on the signs of the Pocahontas Saloon and the post office, which was also the general store. A second look at the store told me that the telegraph went to it, because I saw an overhead wire. If she wanted to, Mother could send a telegram that we were here on a clicker key to Mr. Wallace. Then he would know she'd been able to do the job!

Women and men came out onto the porches of the general store, saloon, and houses to stare at us. I shaded my eyes from the sun with one hand to look at them. I hunted for Phipennys among them but didn't see any. Good. Joshua was safe then.

Mother cried out, "We're from the Monterey library! We've brought the books you wanted."

"The devil and Tom Walker! The library's here!" screeched one woman, who came running down off the general-store porch.

"Our books?" cried another, who rushed toward us from the front door of a little house.

The first one was a scrawny little lady with wispy orange hair twisted up into a knot on top of her head. She had on a brown dress that looked as if had been made out of gunnysacks. The other one was a heavy-set, gray-haired lady in a long red calico skirt and a man's collarless shirt.

I heard Mother call to them, "Are you the ladies who wrote the Monterey library for books?"

"We sure are," yelled the woman in the calico skirt. "I'm Addie Parsons, and this is my friend Marie Simkins. She's the postmistress and clerk in the general store, and she works the telegraph, too. We're sure glad to see ya come!" Addie Parsons wrinkled up her brown face and pointed at the Possum. "Even if you got that old Gil Turlock with ya!"

He told her slowly, "I ain't stayin' here, Addie."

"Glad to hear it." Addie Parsons turned at once to Mother. "Well, liberry lady, who would you be?"

"Mrs. Lettie Ashmore." Then Mother introduced Eubie, me, and Joshua. "Where are the other three ladies who wrote the sheriff for books?" she asked.

The two women looked at one another, and Addie Parsons laughed. "There ain't any more! It's only the two of us."

Mother exclaimed, "But there were five signatures on the letter you wrote. I saw five names on it."

"Oh, that." Marie Simkins waved a little hand as if to brush away a mosquito. "Oh, law, us two signed our own names and made up three more so's the sheriff would think there was more of us up here who was 'desperate.'"

"But why?" The question popped out of me.

Both of them turned their heads to me, then looked away. "We figured folks down where you are might ignore just two desperate ladies in the hills," Marie Simkins said to Mother, "but they'd be sure to listen to five of 'em."

Glory be, the library had been hoodwinked!

Addie Parsons didn't even look embarrassed. "All right, Marie," she said. "I'll put these liberry folks up tonight in my place, and you take 'em tomorrow. We don't want them to think we don't know what politeness is after their long trip."

Mother said, "Thank you, both, but you need not do that. We have our own tents and supplies."

"But ya got to eat with us, turn and turn about!" said Marie Simkins.

Mother said, "If you wish, thank you." She turned to the Possum, who had not said a word. "Let's set up our camp close to town, so people can come to us for books." I knew that she meant to talk to the two "desperate" ladies later on, asking one of them to be a library outpost.

Turlock said, "Yes, ma'am, and once I do that for ya I'll be off on my own bus'ness."

Bold as brass, Eubie asked him, "Who's that business of yours to be with, Possum?"

"Folks I know in a valley some distance away. It's a place where a hound with a foot-long nose couldn't find me. I plan to hunt up the Gordons and settle things between us."

The Gordons? I felt the hairs prickling on the back of my neck. Sure as could be, Turlock was going away to feud. Was that why he had the pistol?

I saw that the two ladies were staring at him with slack jaws as he rode past them.

Marie Simkins exclaimed, "He's actually goin' to look up them Gordons! He's took leave of his senses since he's been away in jail."

Addie Parsons sniffed. "He never could have had any real sense in the first place to marry one of 'em, even if Amy Gordon used to be a mighty pretty girl."

I rode Blackie up to Mother and said in a low voice, "Try to talk the Possum out of what he plans to do."

She gave me her "keep quiet" look, nudged Brownie with her toe, and rode past me, following Turlock, Eubie, Joshua, and all the mules.

As we went by Addie Parsons shouted out, "There'll be fried spring rooster at my house tonight at six o'clock. It's the one with the honeysuckle vine on the front. Marie'll be there too, once she closes up the post office, so we can talk to you about the books you brung us. We got a letter from the liberry man in Monterey, sayin' you want to set up a lendin' liberry here."

So the ladies had been told by mail what else Mother was here for. That was good.

Cupping her hands to her mouth, Marie Simkins

169

called, "Addie and me talked it over earlier, and we think the women's and kids' books ought'a be in the general store and the gents' books in the saloon."

Just like Pickett's Crossing! I looked at Mother and saw her shoulders sag. Now she and Addie Parsons and Marie Simkins would have to go through the saddlebags and choose what books would go where. Her work would have been easier if she could have left them all together.

As I passed the Pocahontas Saloon, a bright idea struck me. No gent who went in there would be upset by a book smelling of whiskey. Somehow, by hook or by crook, I was going to try to get our hoodoo Poe book into the ones that would go to the saloon. If the absolute worst came to the absolute worst, I'd get hold of it secretly and toss it in over the top of the swinging doors as we rode out of Big Tree Junction on our return trip to Monterey. There was one advantage to being the last in line; nobody would see me do it. I'd be glad to repay the library for the book out of my allowance, if I had to.

The Possum set up our camp for us a little distance behind the general store. Afterward he went aside with Mother and, standing beneath a sycamore, talked with her for quite a while. I couldn't hear what they said, but I saw him tip his hat to her, turn about, and stride away onto a path that led downhill into tall timber.

I ran up to her. "You couldn't get him to stay here?"

"No, Fayette." Her face was solemn. "He has business elsewhere."

"What about a feud, Mother? Is that his business?"

She shook her head. "He really doesn't know if there's

170

a feud going on between him and his wife's family or not. He does suspect that the Gordons bear him some ill will, though, and wants to talk to them about things. His wife's brother was the one who started the fight, not Turlock."

I asked, "If they aren't too mad at him, will he stay up here with his wife?"

"He doesn't know, but he told me that after eight years he feels that he's probably not much fit for wedded life anymore. He says he likes the wilderness and being alone. He felt 'close packed' in prison."

I asked, "Will he go wild again up here?"

"No, he says he prefers the country around the Mackenzie homestead." She smiled at me.

"But will he go back to Monterey with us when we're ready to leave?"

"I don't know, Fayette, but I hope so. Any arrangement I have with him is a very loose one. He wouldn't take any money from me now for guiding us to Big Tree Junction, since he wanted to come here in any event and see the people he left behind. He wants to talk to his wife and see if he can do anything for her because of her brother. He feels a sense of obligation. I could not budge him with any argument."

I thought about how he'd helped us camp on the trail, how he'd got Shem up out of the ravine, how he'd dug the grave for the Rogers boy, and how he'd sat on a log with little birds all around him. He'd been a help to us and a help to the library. I'd figured him wrong just because of the way he looked and talked. "You know, I guess I judged a book by its cover," I told Mother.

171

"Yes, Fayette. It's easy to do." She pulled me to her to hug me briefly, then let me go.

"What if he doesn't ever come back? What'll we do?"

"Try to hire a mule skinner here, and if that fails, I'll telegraph Mr. Wallace to hire someone to come up here to take us back to Monterey. I'm not willing to attempt that journey with Eubie as our muleteer, are you? We'll wait three days here for Mr. Turlock to come back before I telegraph. I promised to give him that much time."

I said, "If he doesn't come back, we can telegraph the sheriff to come up and find out what happened to him."

"We could, Fayette, but he asked me to leave him alone."

I said, "That isn't fair!" and would have said more, but just at that moment Eubie came hurtling up to us.

"Hey, Josh got a job right off!" he exploded. "He's going to live above the saloon and sweep out the place. He won't be coming back with us. He says it looks like a good job. The saloonkeeper's an old gink who says he's been looking for a boy to help him for a whole year."

"Eubie, you've been inside the saloon?" accused Mother.

"Sure, I went in with Josh!" A broad grin creased Eubie's face. "And it was just like it is in the cowboy movies."

Mother told him dryly, "All right. Now that you have seen a saloon, you don't need to see another one."

Eubie's face fell. Then he looked around our campsite and asked, "Where's the Possum?"

"Gone home to his wife," I told him, "or maybe gone feuding."

"He didn't say good-bye to me!"

"He didn't say good-bye to me either, just to Mother."

"Well, I'm going to talk to him before he leaves. Which way did he go, Fayette?"

I pointed downhill and said what the cowboys always said in movies, "He went thataway a couple of minutes ago. If you go fast, you can head him off at the pass."

"*Adios*," cried Eubie, and without asking Mother's permission he started to run down the trail Turlock had taken.

Where did Eubie get all his pep? I was very weary and felt as if I might fall over where I stood. "I'm sure tired," I told Mother.

"Oh, Fayette, so am I. It's the altitude here. We are higher up than we have ever been before." She took in a deep breath and cried, "The air is wonderful, even if it makes me giddy." Then she said, looking at me, "You know, Fayette, you've grown. You can look eye-to-eye with me now, can't you?" I nodded, and she went on. "We've done it! We've met problems as they came up and dealt with them. We got up here in one piece with the books. I think I could have done it by myself even if Mr. Turlock had not come back to us."

"Mother, could you have shot the mule?"

"Yes, Fayette, I could have, and somehow I would have got us turned around and on the right way to Big Tree Junction. If I don't get a job at the Monterey li-

173

brary when we get home, I'll find another job somewhere else. If we have to sell our house to survive until I find library work, we'll do that. I think we're all stronger than we were. This trip has given me an unexpected, personal gain. It's increased my courage as well as stretched my muscles. I am certain now that I will not marry Mr. Herbert."

I contented myself with saying, "We've got some confidence in ourselves now." Then I volunteered, "I'm out of school now. I could go to work to help us out, I guess. I could work in a fish cannery."

"Yes, you could do that, but I want you to go to school and then on to a higher education."

I told her, "High school could wait if it has to."

"Thank you, Fayette. Thank you." She gave me a second hug, then said, her smile fading, "I only wish I didn't have the matter of Mr. Turlock on my mind so very much."

"He isn't only on *your* mind, Mother. He's on mine, too, and he's sure on Eubie's to make him chase after him. I think Eubie was taking to him."

"He surely was. I believe the Possum was a good man for Eubie to get to know at this stage in his life."

Being at Addie Parson's house for supper that night was surely an odd experience, even if I was getting sort of used to odd happenings up in the hills.

Her house was the barest one I'd ever been in. Though it had a parlor and bedroom and kitchen, there was hardly any furniture in it except for a bed, a kitchen and parlor stove, a round table, four rickety chairs, two

174

nail kegs, and a rocking chair. And she'd said that she'd put us Ashmores up! No rugs, no curtains, no sofa, nothing. There was a white-bearded old gink, who sat silently in the rocking chair, rocking with his hat on. He never said a word while Addie Parsons and Marie Simkins talked before supper about library business with Mother.

I looked around in vain for any books, though I knew the desperate ladies were supposed to have six of them. There was a little corner bookshelf, but there was nothing on it, not even a bud vase.

Mother was not only outnumbered by the two Big Tree Junction women but outplanned. They had already figured out how to run the library outposts. They'd got permission from the saloon owner to circulate books from his place, and they'd already arranged for the hours of library business and who would be on duty where. Addie Parsons would work in the saloon, because saloons didn't "upset" her. Marie Simkins, as postmistress, would be the librarian in the general store. She said lots of people came there from out of the hills. She promised to send everyone who bought anything away with books, and Addie Parsons had decided that "every galoot who came in for a snort of whiskey would go home with some readin' matter."

As I sat on my keg beside Eubie, I wondered about the bearded man, asking myself if he was Mr. Parsons. Addie Parsons must have seen me looking at him, because all at once she gestured toward him and said, "That old slump's my brother, Hezekiah. He's so lazy he never scratched unless what bit him bit hard, and he ain't much for conversing, so don't expect him to talk to ya. He's stone deaf to boot, so he don't even jump when I get after 'it.' The devil and Tom Walker, I think mebbe I hear the cussed thing right this very minute!"

Up she jumped and ran into the kitchen. I saw her reach to the side of the door, pull out a rifle, aim, and shoot in the direction of the wood piled up against the outhouse. *Bam, bam,* two shots in a row!

Marie Simkins sang out from her chair without turning around, "Did ya get him, Addie dear?"

"No, cuss the luck, he got away agin!"

"Are ya sure ya don't want me to let my kitty out to help ya?" Mrs. Simkins wanted to know. "It'd be in his nature."

"The devil and Tom Walker, no, Marie. I won't let my grit weaken. I'll get it in time, the way I did that ornery cougar that used to walk through town at sunset when Hezekiah and me came here in 1900. I shot some bears then too. . . ."

"What is *it?*" interrupted Eubie, as interested as I was.

As she put the rifle away, Addie said, "A wood rat, sonny. A wood rat as long as yer leg and livin' in my firewood. Well, maybe I'll still get it before the light gets too bad tonight. Marie, you keep the liberry folks comp'ny while I build the biscuits." And she shut the kitchen door.

Mother asked, "So we are having biscuits then?"

"That isn't what it sounds like, missus. Addie only means she's fixin' grub for us all."

"Oh," said Mother.

176

Then Marie Simkins asked, "How come you're travelin' with that Gil Turlock?"

Mother, who had surely been expecting this question, drew a deep breath and told about Mr. Murfree's accident and our linking up with Turlock. She told the woman that she knew of his prison record and that he'd been of "enormous help" to us and to the library. She said that she hoped he would come back to take us down to Monterey, and if he didn't, we'd need a mule skinner from Big Tree Junction. I thought Mother explained everything very well.

Her face twisting up as she listened, Marie Simkins said at the very end, "There ain't no mule skinners hereabouts that I know of. Maybe you'd best figger on telegraphin' the sheriff in Monterey right away."

Mother said calmly, "No, I plan to wait for Mr. Turlock for a time." Then she asked the question that was bothering me. "Where are Miss Parson's books? I presume she has some of the six you wrote about."

"Sure, they're over at my house. It's my month to have 'em in my special Sir Walter corner."

"Sir Walter corner?" asked Mother.

"Sir Walter Scott corner. I got a picture of him and two of his books about knights and castles and fightin'."

Mother said, "I see. You and Miss Parsons take turns having the books?"

"Uh-huh, it gives us somethin' to look at. I got my two Scotts, her Bible, her *Robinson Crusoe* and *Uncle Tom's Cabin*, and my Edgar Allan Poe book."

Poe? I asked, "Poe?" hoping she only had his poems, not his stories.

"You bet. I got all the stories he wrote."

My heart sank just as I heard *bam, bam* from the kitchen and a yell, "I missed him again, Marie."

Afterward we made polite talk with Mrs. Simkins, who was a widow lady. We talked about the war in Europe, which she'd heard about but was confused over. Then as we had with the Mackenzie women, we talked about movies, which she'd never seen, and about Charlie Chaplin, Mary Pickford, and the vampire lady, Theda Bara. Mother talked about white elephant parties that got rid of things nobody wanted and about the mandolin club she might join in the winter.

All at once, we heard a queer buzzing, coughing sound from outside that made Mrs. Simkins let out a cry. "Addie, it's come back again!"

Another "it?" The kitchen door flew open and out came Miss Parsons, wearing a flour sack over her calico skirt but without the rifle. She and Mrs. Simkins dashed out the front door, leaving it wide open. Forgetting Hezekiah Parsons in his rocker, we Ashmores ran after them and stood next to the big tree looking up into the twilight sky.

In an instant, we learned the cause of the noise. An airplane. The most modern thing in all of California was up here in Big Tree Junction! It was a little silver-and-scarlet airplane flying over us, its propeller whirling, its wings dipping to let us know our waves had been seen.

We kept on waving until the plane circled again and then flew off to the north toward San Francisco.

178

"Good heavens!" marveled Mother. "I'd never expected to see an airplane way up here. The aviator must be a very brave or very foolish man. There's no place at all to land up here if he has trouble with his engine." She asked Mrs. Simkins, "Do planes come here often?"

"Not often, they don't. Ain't it queer, though, missus? We got no roads. I never even seen a automobile except in a magazine that got sent up here in the mail. But I seen an airplane four times now."

As we walked back to the house, Addie Parsons turned to me and asked with a smile, "Honey, do you know any of the new songs down in Monterey?"

I said, "I know 'From the Land of Sky Blue Waters.' It's a new one, I think. We have a record of it that we play on our victrola at home."

"Would you kindly sing it for us after supper?"

I looked at Mother unhappily, and she said, "Of course, Fayette will be happy to sing it."

Happy I would not be, but I would sing it, and so I did after a fine supper of fricasseed chicken that was interrupted only once by Miss Addie's taking another shot at the woodpile wood rat and missing again. She just wasn't as good a shot as Malindy Mackenzie Culpepper.

After a peaceful night in our own tents and after tending to the mules and Hagar in the morning, Mother, Eubie, and I opened the saddlebags and set the books on the ground. Then Mother told me to go ask the desperate ladies to come and choose their books.

They came right away. Oh, how they loved those

books! I saw how they picked them up, caressed their spines, and opened them with great care. They loved every slow minute and every single page.

They took most of the day to go through the books and separate them into piles for the general store and saloon. Of course, I watched carefully for our hoodoo book to come up, and to my great joy I saw Addie Parsons examine it and put it with the ones for the saloon.

But somehow Marie Simkins wasn't satisfied with that pile and went through it again. To my disgust, she hauled out the Poe book saying, "This here wouldn't get read by anybody up here. There ain't a soul but me who could read the stories of Poe, and I already got him and read him. You'd best take this one back with you, Missus Ashmore."

"All right, if you think so," agreed Mother, who I thought was being too agreeable.

"Not all right!" I whispered under my breath.

Afterward the books went as they had in Pickett's Crossing by wheelbarrow to the general store and saloon. Marie Simkins pushed one barrow to the store and Addie Parsons the other to the Pocahontas Saloon.

Mother put Poe's tales back into the now-empty saddlebag, but it didn't stay there long. I had another idea for it, a better one than throwing it over the saloon doors.

When we went to Mrs. Simkins' for supper that night, "The Fall of the House of Usher" went with me under my shirt, stuck in my belt. It wasn't comfortable sitting down with it there, but it was something I had to do.

That was quite an evening too. Again we ate chicken, which seemed to be the one thing mountain people wanted to feed company. I guessed they didn't think of squirrel or bear as any treat, because they had it so often, but I would have preferred some wilderness food.

Mrs. Simkins' house was so full of stuff I could hardly find a place to sit down in it. She was a weaver. There was a spinning wheel, rag rugs, a lumpy sofa, seven chairs, a table, and a large loom in the parlor. Her dress wasn't made of gunnysack but homespun wool, which came from sheep raised nearby. We all admired her Sir Walter Scott corner, with the picture of the author in a golden frame and the six books grouped around it, three on each side of Scott. Her copy of Poe's tales was bound in very dark-blue leather and was at the right of the right-hand group books.

Eubie, who had enjoyed Addie Parsons' shooting at the wood rat, asked right after we sat down in Mrs. Simkins' parlor, "Where's your kitty? Can I see it?"

"Oh, law, the Little One, my pet kitty cat," she exclaimed, throwing up her hands. "I keep Little One in the woodbox on the back porch."

I asked, "In the woodbox?"

Addie Parsons leaned back in her chair and chuckled. "Marie has to. Little One's still a little wild, but what else can ya expect out of a baby wildcat?"

"A wildcat?" Eubie was naturally delighted with that idea. "Can I see it?"

"Sure ya can," agreed Mrs. Simkins. "You and yer sister can go out through my kitchen and onto the back porch. Lift up the top of the woodbox carefully. Look in the box, but don't put yer hand down inside it. Little One ain't to be patted, not yet anyways."

"Mebbe never," prompted Miss Parsons. "Marie didn't have any luck with her last wildcat. It wouldn't eat and upped and died on her."

"Little One's different. It's got a nicer nature. I think it's a female, but I'm not sure yet," said Mrs. Simkins. "It's more loving, I'd say. It eats raw meat just fine."

I got up with Eubie, went out to the kitchen, and stayed there when he went out onto the back porch. I could see a solid-built woodbox with a hinged top in the corner. "Now you be careful!" I said to Eubie.

He didn't listen to me any better than he ever did. While I stood in the doorway, he grabbed hold of the lid and lifted it up fast instead of slowly.

Out boiled a big, yellowish-brown animal, all claws, teeth, and snarls. It sprang past Eubie's shoulder straight for me and tried to attack me in the stomach. Just in time I leaped aside, as Little One streaked past me into the parlor in a terrible burst of speed.

What a horrible racket came out of the parlor—yelling and shriekings, snarlings and growlings. I clutched at my stomach, feeling Edgar Allan Poe there.

My chance! Here it was at last! I ran into the parlor and saw Mother up on the sofa. Addie Parsons and Mrs. Simkins were trying to catch Little One, Addie with a crocheted afghan and Marie with a purple shawl. Naturally, nobody was paying one bit of attention to me.

I ran over to Sir Walter's corner, whipped the book out from under my shirt, grabbed Mrs. Simkins' Poe, and put the library copy in its place. Her book I tucked back into my shirt.

As Addie Parsons screeched, "I got it in your comforter, Marie!" I congratulated myself on having got rid of "The Fall of the House of Usher" at last.

Though it put up an awful tussle, the wildcat got shoved back into its woodbox and Eubie got scolded by Mother for having opened it so hastily.

Afterward things were peaceful enough, though it didn't appear to me that the ladies appreciated the poem I'd learned at school as an assignment from Miss Uffelman. I recited it to them instead of singing another song.

I only got partway through it, reciting just the lines:

"O crocodile, I never thought till now
To pen a sonnet to the likes of you
But since a sonnet has been written to
All else on earth, I will, if you'll allow
Entwine about your corrugated brow
This wreath of rhyme . . . ."

I recited the rest of it to Mother and Eubie on our way back to our tents after supper, because the desperate ladies told me they didn't like modern poems.

Mother seemed absentminded as she looked up at the stars that seemed close enough to touch way up here in the hills.

I remarked, "The desperate ladies are sort of odd, aren't they? Shooting at wood rats and trying to tame wildcats?"

Mother said, "You might be odd too, Fayette, if you lived up here in the wilds with only six books and no other entertainment. Don't you see that getting that wood rat and taming the wildcat are challenges to these poor women? Perhaps now that they have books to read they won't find such matters so important. I trust that the wood rat will enjoy a good, long, peaceful life and the poor wildcat will be released."

She paused and spoke again. "As for us, I wonder how Mr. Turlock is doing. My work's done here for the library. I do hope he will be back tomorrow evening." She sighed. "I don't want to wait up here for a week or so while the library sends us another muleteer. I asked around town and have found that there simply aren't any men here able and willing to lead us back to Monterey. I will wait for Mr. Turlock until near sundown tomorrow, and then I'll send a telegram to Mr. Wallace to get a mule skinner for us. But I'd prefer to have Mr. Wallace think that things went very smoothly for us here in the mountains."

I asked, "Will we eat with the desperate ladies again?"

"No. They both asked us, but we'll fix our own meals. I find the shooting a bit hard on my nerves, and I'm sorry for the wildcat."

My conscience bothered me that night about taking Mrs. Simkins' copy of the Poe book. Furthermore, I wasn't sure I wanted to take any copy of that book back to Monterey with us. It might be too risky. So the next morning in the general store, while Mother and Mrs. Simkins were busy, I slipped Mrs. Simkins' copy among the library books on the shelf. Let her find it after we'd

184

left town! If somebody wanted to check it out, she'd be sure to see that it was her copy.

That happy chore done, I went out on the porch of the general store. As I was sitting there dreaming, Eubie and Joshua passed me, carrying one of our blankets.

I yelled to my brother, "What're you up to?"

"We got something to do." Eubie was being mysterious. Well, let him.

I said, "Okay, do it, but don't get into any trouble."

Sitting on the long bench in the warm afternoon sunshine, I almost fell asleep. Then suddenly I heard Mother's voice from behind me.

She said, "What on earth is that, Mrs. Simkins? Is it a forest fire? Is it Indians?"

Indians? A forest fire? I sat up with a start.

Marie Simkins was saying, "There ain't any Indians up here now, but those sure do appear to be smoke signals. No, they ain't from a fire."

I shaded my eyes with my hands and looked out beyond the big tree. Yes, there they were, big blobs of gray smoke, rising above one another and into the blue sky.

Suddenly I knew what they were, and I grinned. Apparently Eubie had been hiding a real secret when he'd acted so mysterious. I told Mother and Mrs. Simkins, "Oh, it's only Eubie and Joshua."

Mother sounded exasperated. "What are they doing? Do you know, Fayette?"

"Just playing Indian. Joshua won't let Eubie set the mountains on fire. They'll be back before sunset."

They did come back, and they didn't come alone. With a boy on each side of him, the Possum lumbered toward us as we sat at our campfire. Alive and un-wounded by any feud, he'd come back. He was as big and as shaggy as ever, and I knew in my heart he was ready to go to Monterey with us. His business with his wife and her family was over with!

Mrs. Simkins, who was having coffee with Mother, saw the Possum too. She said disgustedly, "Oh, it's that danged pesky Gil Turlock back again!"

"Yes, oh, yes, it *is* Mr. Turlock!" cried Mother, who leaped up from where she was sitting and ran off to meet him and the two boys. I stayed where I was with Mrs. Simkins but said nothing to her.

Sure as could be before Turlock left, he and Eubie had arranged a signal that would tell the Possum if we needed him badly.

Knowing Turlock, I doubted if we'd ever find out how things had gone for him, but that was all right too. He was back with us now, so I kept quiet while Mrs. Simkins tramped away, muttering about how bad he was.

Joshua Drucker had supper with us our last night in Big Tree Junction. Afterward Mother told him, "Joshua, I'll be sure to let the proper county authorities know how the Phipennys treat their orphan boys and where you are living now. I don't think you need have any fears anymore." Then she got her valise and took out the Civil War pistol he'd given to her. She handed it back to him with the words, "Thank you for giving me this, but I'd rather you have it. Please take it back. It's

186

not really the sort of present librarians are fond of, though I know you meant well when you gave it to me."

As Joshua took it, he told her, "Oh, that's all right, ma'am, I'll take it back. I guess I can tell ya now that it wasn't ever loaded. I couldn't get any bullets at Pickett's Crossin' that were the right size for it."

Mother shook her head, sighed, then laughed while she glanced at the Possum, who was looking up at the night sky as if he hadn't heard a word that was said.

I thought our last minutes in Big Tree Junction were both interesting and exciting.

We had a nifty farewell, one that I would never forget. As we all rode out past the general store, Mrs. Simkins, who had said good-bye earlier that morning, came rushing out onto the front porch holding up a skinny, dark-colored book. I thought she looked mad as hops as she waved at us.

Because I knew what the book was, I yelled out at the very same moment she opened her mouth, "Everybody hold onto his reins! Take a deep breath, Eubie. Blow, Eubie, blow!"

Squawk, wah-h-h, squawk went the blast of the Spanish-American War trumpet, and the noises Eubie made covered whatever Mrs. Simkins was shouting at us.

As Blackie started to run, following after Mother's mule, I turned around in my saddle and, glory be, waved good-by to Mrs. Simkins, to "The Fall of the House of Usher," and to our bad luck.

AUTHOR'S NOTE

Eight Mules from Monterey deals with several things that might be of interest to young readers who want to separate fact from my fancy.

Before I started to write for children, I worked on the staffs of public and private libraries in the states of Idaho, Washington, Delaware, and California. These library jobs as a documents clerk in a university library, as a children's librarian, as a science and finally a business librarian have given me, I feel, some insider's knowledge of library functions and of the library profession.

The concept of libraries is an old one. In ancient and medieval times, both individuals and groups of people living together in monasteries and colleges maintained private libraries for themselves. Nineteenth-century libraries often charged membership fees. Libraries that are free of charge, that is, public libraries for "everybody," are a new idea. Even today not all libraries are open to the public, nor do they circulate books. They are for scholars who come with special introductions to enter them. The books stay in the library at all times.

The United States has had free-of-cost libraries circulating books since 1833. Public libraries require librarians to circulate books, keep records of books that are checked out, buy new books, and repair damaged ones.

Nowadays librarians are educated in universities to learn how to do their special kind of work. There are all sorts of librarians—science, reference, medical, art, music, business, industrial, and children's. Would-be librarians attend graduate schools in librarianship and earn special degrees in library science.

Years ago, however, librarians were sometimes educated in small schools of librarianship that were attached to a town's public library. I have written of such a library school, a fictional one, which I have located in the city of Monterey. (My own city, Riverside, California, had just such a school in the first decades of this century.)

Librarians in 1916 didn't have machines to help them check books out to "patrons," the people who borrow books. They used rubber stamps for due dates and wrote out a borrower's name or number on the book cards. It was a slow and awkward process.

Libraries have changed in many ways since the days of World War I. They do not just circulate books nowadays. They also answer telephone reference questions, circulate phonograph records, tapes and films, operate bookmobiles, keep books for the blind, take books to invalids, etc. In many cases the library buildings of today are also used for club meetings, concerts, film showings and as art galleries.

In this book, I have written of what one child I know calls a "mulemobile." Was there such a thing? In a sense, yes. Though my Mrs. Ashmore, Fayette, and

Eubie are fictional, as are their adventures, there was a real Monterey, California, librarian, who, in 1916, rode through the roadless Santa Lucia Mountains to set up library outposts. Her name was Miss Anne Hadden. She was born in Ireland and came to California in 1892. Doing her duty by her library, she did my Ashmores one better. Leaving her mount at one point, Miss Hadden and another stalwart lady hiked over seventy miles of hazardous trails to mountain areas inaccessible by mules or horses. Her heroic efforts established several branch libraries in the mountains, and afterward books went back and forth to the people there by mail.

What I have written of mules is true. Mules are preferred to horses for mountain travel. They are more surefooted, more intelligent than horses, eat less, and are physically more powerful. Unfortunately, they are also renowned for their bad tempers and stubbornness. The mule is an offspring of a female horse and a male donkey. They cannot reproduce themselves. It is said that mules in a pack train will follow a gray or white mare anywhere, even if she is out of sight around a bend in a trail, so long as they can hear a bell she wears around her neck.

Handling mules is considered a high art by people who deal with them. Supposedly, this work requires a combination of respect, cunning, cussing, and enormous patience. Mules are not popular as riding animals today, yet in ancient and medieval times they were highly prized as mounts by kings, bishops, and queens. George

190

Washington was a great fancier of mules and a breeder of fine animals.

Though my account of a mule surviving a fall down a ravine may seem farfetched, it is not. Mules are practically indestructible and far less susceptible to ailments than horses.

The mare Hagar's bout with chills and fatigue and her whiskey-and-oats cure, though unorthodox, could have happened. Some horses are fond of alcohol, I'm told, though I personally have never offered one a drink.

My depiction of the mountain inhabitants around Monterey as an odd lot comes from old familial tales I've heard and from the somber poems and collected letters of the poet Robinson Jeffers, who lived in those hills at one time. Though there were no roads until 1937, the mountains were flown over by planes even in 1916 and were visited by circuit-riding doctors, nurses, and school superintendents. The making of illegal whiskey went on for years, as it did in other mountain regions of the United States. The Sir Walter Scott corner my Marie Simkins maintains is fictional, but there was a real pioneer woman who had a parlor literary corner of her own, dedicated not to Scott but to the American poet Henry Wadsworth Longfellow, a great nineteenth-century favorite. Another pioneer woman was renowned for interrupting her social life by constantly shooting at "critters" in her backyard. The rifle at the back door was a most common feature of American pioneer life.

I have tried as much as possible to give the flavor of

the speech and customs of 1916. *Nifty, classy,* and *gink* were slang words of the day, the poem Fayette recites came from a 1915 issue of *Century* and was written by Oliver Herford, and the song "From the Land of Sky Blue Waters" was a popular hit.

I wish to thank several people for helping me with my research. First comes the Arizona woman who told me over the telephone in 1980 about her woodbox-housed wildcat pet, Little One, giving me permission to put the animal into my next book. The Wild West lives!

For xeroxed material sent me about the actual 1916 trip of the redoubtable Monterey county librarian Anne Hadden, I must convey my deep appreciation to Mrs. Roseellen Graft, reference librarian of the Monterey County Library in Salinas. I hope she and other Monterey county and city librarians will understand my necessary liberties and "fictions." Although the real Miss Hadden did not take a child with her in 1916, I could scarcely write for children without a child character. I am sure, however, that Miss Hadden, who must have been an unflappable librarian in the best library tradition, could have easily dealt with the fictional adventures of my Ashmore family with Irish grace and gallantry and would forgive me for not specifying that the Monterey County Library is the library that sends the Ashmores forth.

Patricia Beatty
March 1981